The Untold Story of Edwina

Also by Lynne Handy

In the Time of Peacocks

Spy Car and Other Poems

The Untold Story of Edwina

Lynne Handy

Push On Press

Dedication

To Morgan, daughter of the lakes

Acknowledgements

I am indebted to Kate Johnson, who helped edit my manuscript; to William Pack, who caught the essence of the novella in his cover design; and to Kevin Moriarity, who patiently formatted the novella for publication.

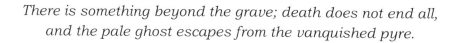

There is something beyond the grave; death does not end all,
and the pale ghost escapes from the vanquished pyre.

(Sextus Aurelius Propertius, *Elegies II*)

Chapter I

Trysting lovers had peopled my dreams; white moons, too, and the blood of charging bulls—consequences of reading Federico García Lorca at bedtime. Now, morning. A mewled dawn crept through my window alerting me to the rise of a yet invisible sun. My feet felt the cold of the hardwood floor, but that was not sufficient to raise me to full consciousness, so I batted around a bit. Mathieu had already risen and gone to teach his early morning class. I lingered over hot chocolate and a melting marshmallow that resembled a fat angel spreading its wings.

I sighed, finally letting go of Lorca's alabaster moons. Today was my colleague Edwina Frost's funeral. As my eyes traveled around the kitchen and into the sunroom, rain began to trickle down the screens. Klimt masterpieces, I thought, watching raindrops pulse in the mesh like sequins on silk. Why couldn't I stay home and write a rainy day poem? I hated funerals. I hated rainy funerals more. Dickenson's immortal words chastened me.

> Good night, because we must
> How intricate the dust!
> I would go, to know!
> Oh, incognito!

In a few hours, I'd see Edwina lowered into the ground. Not yet time to know my own death, but I felt its predatory graze.

Pulling myself together, I showered and dressed. The television news crawl spun out its dreary message—rain to continue all day. The next announcement caught my eye. A tile digger had dug up a child's skeleton near Sugar Creek in Prophet County. How very disturbing and sad. Trusting the evening paper to provide details, I grabbed a black handbag and hurried to my car.

Fog from the Wabash River webbed the streets as I drove to the cathedral—Edwina *would* warrant a cathedral! Murk stalked the day like her macabre works of fiction, Poe-like in their telling of men and women crazed by guilt. I hadn't known Edwina well. Had anyone? We both taught at the university. Our offices were in the same building, though not on the same floor. We hadn't seen each other daily or even weekly.

I drove through downtown Fennville, now mostly law firms and banks. A few years ago, department stores and shops moved to malls off highways that surrounded the city. The Episcopal cathedral loomed before me and I parked in a lot near the exit. I didn't plan to visit the gravesite. I had work to complete; a celebratory ode for the birthday of Sasha Rice, a nonagenarian poet revered by the English Department, and a lecture to prepare on Pound.

As I approached the cathedral doors, a deep, masculine voice said, "Maria Pell."

Edwina's nephew, Hugh Bentley, hurried toward me, his lips upturned in a politician's grin. I liked Hugh. An attorney, he possessed a good mind. He was handsome, fortyish, and had a pillowed chin with a cleft like Lord Byron. We had served on several committees together. In the next election, he planned to run for the state senate seat. As far as I knew, he'd make a fine legislator. We embraced and he fell in step beside me. After we exchanged quiet words about Edwina, he surprised me by asking a question.

"Would you like to write a biography of Aunt Edwina?"

I blinked. "I'm a poet, Hugh. I've never written biography."

"I've read your committee reports. You write well and I need someone I can trust. You probably know I'm running for office next term. Aunt Edwina had a few...quirks...and I wouldn't want her story told without understanding. You'd be more sympathetic than a stranger."

"Quirks?" I paused to consider the word. It was true that Edwina was unsociable—occasionally rude—but weren't most creative people subject to melt-downs? I certainly had my down days.

He touched my arm. "You knew her, Maria, and you're also a writer."

"Oh, I don't know, Hugh. Let me think about it."

"Don't take too long. The moment I announce my candidacy, someone's bound to start looking for dirt about her. She was, after all, the Queen of Horror Fiction. I want a sensible biography out before that happens."

I smiled. Years ago, a reviewer had crowned Edwina the indisputable master of her genre. But I wondered about Hugh's concern. Edwina had been an eccentric woman, slave to raw emotions, but I doubted anyone could find *dirt* about her.

We joined a group of mourners, so halted our conversation and entered the somberly-lit church; he, stopping to wait with family members for the hearse, and I, taking a seat close to the door. A few minutes later, the organist played the first notes of Mascagni's "Intermezzo" as acolytes entered the nave bearing torches and a cross. Pall bearers followed with the coffin, walking stiffly to the head of the nave and lowering it onto a trestle. The bishop, a white cope tied over his cassock, began the funeral liturgy.

I thought of Edwina Frost, who had died at eighty-five, reportedly from a stroke. A tall thin woman, possibly attractive in her youth, she had aged badly, the corners of her mouth sagging, and deep, unhappy crevices forming between her eyebrows.

Hugh's comment about her quirks stayed with me. As the service progressed, I tried to recall rumors I'd heard. People on a neighboring farm had notified the police about mistreated dogs, but whatever happened, the talk died down. When the Frost land was sold, Edwina had a fistfight with her sister, Louise Bentley, Hugh's socialite mother. Edwina had attempted to block the sale, but the courts allowed Louise to sell her half. A photographer had caught the courthouse scene: Edwina pummeling Louise, who held up a Gucci purse as a shield. The photograph had landed on the front page of the local newspaper. Weeks later, Edwina published a short story about a woman who carved up her sister like a Smithfield ham.

I looked up as Hugh stood to eulogize his aunt, delivering his remarks with no amusing asides. Quite possibly, there were none for him to remember. He spoke about Edwina's dedication to teaching and writing, and her success as a novelist.

The choir sang a hymn with a melismatic passage. My thoughts returned to the biography. If I agreed to write it and my research uncovered dark deeds, Hugh would expect me to conceal them. But what was I thinking? Edwina, like me, poured her deepest stresses into her writing. Didn't the Smithfield ham prove that?

I'd last seen Edwina a month ago, near the river. Mathieu

and I had taken Fritzi, our spaniel, for a walk, and were arguing over Kathleen Raine's poem, "Into What Pattern." Mathieu looked fabulous in a leather cape slung over a green and gold dashiki. He stunned people—particularly women—with his brown skin, tall stature, and well-muscled build. That day, he'd taken the position that the poem was an example of the freeing-up that occurred after Eliot wrote his essay on tradition and talent. I thought the poem stultifying and compared it to a ship in a bottle.

"The music of the spheres controls all the action," I said.

At that point, Edwina passed us without speaking.

"Edwina," I called.

She turned, her face pinched with irritation. "Leave me alone," she snapped.

"Well," I said.

Mathieu shrugged. "Perhaps she's not feeling well. She's getting on in years."

I watched her stomp off. She'd been wearing a dark trench coat. With dyed black hair slicked by rain, she'd looked like a half-drowned crow.

A bell tinkled. The Kontakion. I looked toward the altar. "*Give rest, O Christ, to your servant,*" intoned the priest. Unexpectedly, I shivered and then the oddest thing happened—I felt moisture on both cheeks, as if tears had fallen from my eyes. I touched my face with my fingertips and they came away wet.

Hormones, no doubt, playing tricks on me again. I was forty; they ebbed and flowed, confusing my system.

The organist burst into *Jesu, Joy of Man's Desiring,* startling me. Pallbearers bore Edwina's remains back to the hearse. As I stepped in the aisle, I saw Mathieu, handsome in a dark suit, standing near the door.

"Did you wear socks?" I whispered.

It was a running battle between us. He hated socks. I thought it unsanitary not to wear them.

"You know I never do."

"Not even to a funeral?"

"Not even to funerals." He kissed my cheek. "Shall we go to the cemetery?"

I opened my mouth to say no, but something edged me into indecision. It had to do with wondering what Mathieu wanted to do, for I usually deferred to him. He was five years my junior, and though he was the most constant of lovers, I sometimes worried he would leave me for a younger woman— an agony that manifested whenever I felt vulnerable. Death, rain, Hugh's proposition—I was off-balance.

"We might as well go," he said. "We'll take my car."

He put his hand on my arm and guided me to his five-year-old Buick. His touch steadied me.

I fastened my seatbelt. "Hugh Bentley asked me to write Edwina's biography."

"That might be interesting. Have you decided to do it?"

"I doubt I'd have authorial control. He worries that Edwina had dark secrets and wants them, as he put it, addressed with understanding of her artistic temperament."

Mathieu put the car into gear. "You're a poet. I wonder why he chose you."

"Hugh often acts spontaneously. Perhaps he'd been wondering what to do about Edwina's legacy and looked up and saw me."

Mathieu smiled. "Serendipity. Much of life is like that."

The rain stopped and we drove through trees still dripping with moisture. By the time we reached Eastland Cemetery, the sun broke through, spreading a pale green haze over the graves. An embryonic poem formed in my mind: *misted years, bones of the dead, a child who*—I jotted down thoughts in the red notebook I carried in my purse.

Mathieu parked along the gravel road and we walked to the grave. The family—what there was of it—had assembled under a gray awning. Hugh sat next to his widowed mother, Mrs. William Bentley, nee Louise Frost, who was dry-eyed. She wore a rose suit and matching hat, hardly mourning attire, but given her history with her sister, she may not have been grieving. Behind Louise sat a man in a poorly-made suit with graying hair falling to his shoulders, whom I vaguely recognized. A cousin, perhaps. I thought I'd seen him at a department picnic held at Edwina's farm. He was weeping. At least someone was expressing sadness at Edwina's passing. Hugh motioned for us to sit beneath the canopy. I touched Mathieu's sleeve and we moved toward vacant chairs.

"My partner," I said, "Mathieu Joubert."

Mathieu took Louise's hand and offered his condolences, then shook hands with Hugh. Hugh introduced us to the older man, Edwina's and Louise's cousin, James Hawthorne. When he lowered his handkerchief, he revealed bright blue eyes like many people of Scandinavian descent. For a few minutes, we discussed the weather in hushed tones.

Then Mathieu spoke up. "If Maria agrees to write Dr. Frost's biography, will she have authorial control?"

Louise bent across Hugh. "We'd have final approval, of course. We can't have just anything printed about Edwina."

Though I usually resented Mathieu speaking for me, I was glad for it this time. His question not only brought to the fore the matter of authorial control, it also showed the extent of Louise's involvement.

"Too many cooks in the kitchen," I said, smiling. "You'll need to find someone else."

Hugh frowned at his mother. "We wouldn't censor Maria.

The most we could ask is for her to inform us if her research turns up anything questionable about Aunt Edwina."

Louise harrumphed. "This whole idea of writing a book about Edwina is ridiculous."

Hugh turned to me. "Do you agree?"

"Edwina was a writer of some renown," I said slowly. "A doctoral student might focus on her as a subject for dissertation and publish the work in book form."

"God forbid," muttered Louise.

"You *must* do it, Maria" said Hugh. "You knew her. You'd lend more understanding to the project than some grad student out to make a name for herself—or himself."

My mind swirled. I hadn't intended to give Hugh an answer so quickly. Edwina was lying cold on the catafalque and we were discussing terms of her biography, a genre I'd never tried. Yet I was sure I could write her life story—I'd written memoir pieces and lyrical essays. Several how-to books had been written on the subject. I could bone up.

A slap on my left wrist! No one had moved. Was Edwina's spirit nearby? The moisture on my face—the tears—had they been mine or hers? It was, after all, *her* funeral, and if her spirit was roaming, why should it not present itself here and now? The skin on my wrist reddened.

I wasn't afraid. Occasionally, I connected with the spirits of deceased poets. Crossing the bar between real and spirit worlds often resulted in failed attempts to touch—clumsy blows, even pinches and scratches. But it was I who had always sought communion with the dead. This, of course, was the opposite: if these strange happenings were caused by Edwina, *she* was reaching out for *me*. The thought made me slightly uneasy. What did she want?

Mathieu gently nudged me, pulling me from my thoughts. "It might be fun, Maria."

I shook my head to clear it, and then looked at Hugh. "Would I have full access to Edwina's papers?"

He handed me two keys from his coat pocket. "The larger one is for her farmhouse, the other, for her office at the university. We have until the end of the month to get her things out."

"While you're there, Maria, you might as well box up everything," said Louise.

"Mother, we're not hiring Maria to clean out Aunt Edwina's office."

Louise raised her chin, looked away.

Mathieu continued as my agent. "How much will you pay Maria?"

Hugh disclosed a number, which I thought generous. If Mathieu took a leave of absence from his summer course, we could vacation in Tuscany. It seemed a windfall.

"All right," I said. "I'll do it."

"I've already talked to someone at Horowitz and Fine Publishing," said Hugh. "They'll need the finished manuscript before June 1 of next year to get the book out before the election."

"That gives me only a little more than a year," I said.

"The semester is nearly over," reasoned Mathieu. "You're teaching a summer class, but it's on American poets. You've taught it a dozen times before. You'd have time to research and write the first chapters of the book."

I turned to Hugh. "My class load is light for the fall and spring semesters." I thought it through. "I can have it done by the end of May of next year."

"Then it's settled," said Hugh. "I'll draw up a contract tomorrow and email it."

The burial ceremony was brief. Afterward, Mathieu drove me back to the cathedral to fetch my car and I followed him home, reflecting on my rashness in agreeing so quickly to write the biography. I'd long wondered what had fired Edwina's bizarre imagination. What if she *had* done something terrible?

Once home, Mathieu picked up the newspaper from the driveway and brought it inside, then took Fritzi for a walk. I scanned the front page, finding an article about the dead child, alongside a photograph of a toy truck found in the metal box with his bones. Authorities speculated the remains were that of a year-old boy, who died from multiple blows to the head and had been in the ground for between fifty and sixty years. The skeleton was discovered on Edwina's property.

The reporter had interviewed Hugh who was quoted: *The child has no connection whatsoever to my family. Anyone could have sneaked on the property and dug a grave with no one knowing, and clearly, someone did.*

"The bones of a child were dug up on the Frost property," I said.

Mathieu read over my shoulder. "Perhaps this is the reason Hugh Bentley worries about his aunt's reputation."

I looked at him quickly. "What are you suggesting?"

He shrugged. "Horror fiction writer...body discovered near her house..."

"Coincidence—that's all it can be."

"Isn't it strange no one reported the child missing?"

"Maybe they did. The death happened decades ago."

"Reporters would have looked into old police reports. Isn't the timing interesting? One body laid to rest, while another is dug up."

I opened the refrigerator and took out leftovers for dinner.

Why didn't Hugh tell me he'd been interviewed about the bones?

After dinner, Mathieu left for a meeting and I went online to order books on writing biography. Then I googled *Edwina Frost,* and found her curriculum vitae and stories about the Frost family. Articles spanned several decades. I sat back in my chair and read them all.

Edwina was born in 1929 into a wealthy Chicago family. Her sister, Louise, came into the world eight years later, soon after their father purchased eighteen hundred acres of land in Prophet County. The family relocated there, becoming country gentry.

I paused to reflect. As a native of Prophet County, I was familiar with Edwin Frost's memorial statue on the courthouse grounds. He was called Captain Frost, not due to military rank, but because of his reputation as a captain of industry; he owned steel mills in Chicago and Gary. As a child, I had pondered his marble likeness, finding his knife-edge features frightening. Now I wondered what it had been like to be his child.

I felt a shudder down my spine as I studied an old photograph of the young family. Hormones again? Or was I identifying with eight year old Edwina, who stood grimly in front of her father, with his thick-fingered hands gripping her shoulders. A small, fragile-looking mother, also unsmiling, sat in a wicker chair holding baby Louise.

Fast forwarding, I learned Edwina had earned her bachelor's and master's degrees from Yale, and her PhD from the University of Pennsylvania. *The Rowboat,* her first book of horror fiction, debuted in 1960, and every two years thereafter, she published a new novel. Everything she wrote landed on the *New York Times Bestseller List.* I jotted down significant dates in my notebook.

Known for Hitchcockian tales, Edwina's prose was spare; she knew the adverb was the enemy of the verb. She created metaphors that jerked the reader upright, as in her comparison of testicles to undercooked dumplings. Her protagonists were twisted; her villains, monsters. I once asked her the source of her ideas and she had answered sourly, "Observing humans devour each other."

More than once, it had occurred to me that Edwina must have been devoured by someone or something. Now I wondered if it had been her father. Turning off the computer, I went downstairs, wrapped myself in an afghan, and watched a televised documentary on the Civil War.

I couldn't help but think about Hugh's dreading someone would dig up dirt on his aunt. What had he sensed inspired her to write her demonic tales? I thought of her again on that rainy day at the river, her sharp tongue, malevolent gaze...

What was it like, journeying through life, hating everyone? The night grew colder. The lights blinked and I wondered if there was a storm close by. Pulling the afghan to my chin, I tried to return my attention to the documentary. General Grant was defeating Pemberton's army at Vicksburg.

Chapter II

When the biography books arrived, I paged through them quickly. Plutarch recommended realism in reconstructing people's lives. Others cautioned against imposing current thought on events of the past. Edwina and I lived contemporaneously—no worry there. Biographer Fawn Brodie's treatment of Thomas Jefferson intrigued me. It was she who proposed that her subject had sired Sally Hemmings's children. To support her theory, Brodie dug deep into Hemmings's life, using dates of her pregnancies, the whereabouts of Jefferson at times of conception, and DNA from descendants. While I admired her in-depth study, I had committed to completing the manuscript in fifteen months and had no time for extensive research. I'd have to do the best I could within a limited amount of time.

On Saturday, I visited Edwina's office in the Humanities Building. As the door slammed shut behind me, I shivered. How empty places of the dead felt! The blinds were drawn, so I turned on the light. A print of Munch's *The Scream* hung over her desk. Had she put it there to intimidate her students? What a perverse sense of humor Edwina had!

She'd been fond of jasmine and the scent still drenched the room. I sneezed. Some poets suffered from sensory-defensiveness, in that their brains intensified the five senses to the point of discomfort. I was particularly susceptible to smells and Edwina's perfume irritated my sinuses. I tried to open a window, but they were permanently closed. Breathing shallowly, I tried to ward off a headache.

The answering machine was beeping. I sat down at her desk to press *play.*

Edwina's voice. *Remember to get Sasha a gift* (the ninety-year-old poet's birthday celebration).

I replayed the recording—six words in Edwina's high-pitched, nasal voice—noting the influence of her eastern schooling, a certain clipped enunciation seldom heard on our campus. Edwina, I thought, was your granite-faced father proud of your academic achievements? Your first novels? Would he have preferred you tell stories of virtuous women and good-hearted men?

A sense of hopelessness washed over me as I surveyed the room. No computer; not even a typewriter. Edwina wrote in long hand. Her teaching assistant handled data input. Books were spilled across the desk; another pile leaned against a glass-doored case. I read the spines—archaeology, Blake's poems, Poe, de Sade, Verlaine. Six of Stephen King's novels.

Edwina died before the spring term ended and all her class records had been transferred to another professor. A syllabus lay on top of a bookcase—she'd been teaching Poe. Staring at me from across the room was a ceramic statue of a raven with narrowed amber eyes. I studied it for a moment—then held it in my hands, admiring the glossy black paint, the golden beak. A handsome bird, posed contemplatively, like the Nevermore bird.

I set it back on the table and bent to the task of clearing the top of the desk. As I removed a dictionary, it slid from my hands, landing on my instep.

"Ow!" I cried, sitting on a chair to massage my foot.

At that moment, all the books leaning against the bookcase tumbled to the floor. Had the dictionary falling dislodged the other books? As far as I could see, nothing else could have been the impetus for their fall.

The air in the room changed. The smell of jasmine became overpowering. I sneezed three times. Then I heard a noise, similar to the hum of electrical high wires.

Was Edwina's ghost in the room?

"Edwina," I whispered. "Would you rather I'd go?"

No response.

The air cleared, the sound stopped. Perhaps it had been the heating system in the building. Shaking my head, I removed the rest of the books, uncovering a green blotter. Scrawled in Edwina's bold hand were the words, *formalin, dura,* and *brain bucket.* Autopsy words. She must have captured them on her blotter before inserting them into a story. Five uncapped pens, a stack of notebooks, and three candy bar wrappers lay randomly.

The desk drawers were crammed with books. I swiftly closed them, except for the lower right drawer where a foot-long iron hand with claw-like nails riveted my attention. An ancient weapon of some sort. In *Dangers of the Night,* Edwina had chronicled the life of a ghoulish Chinese warrior regenerated in the soul of a quiet New York City accountant. Had she used the weapon in that novel? Had anyone used it in real life? I frowned at the menacing hand and closed the drawer.

My cell phone rang—Mathieu, whose cheerful tone lent a welcome diversion from my task. We discussed dinner and chatted for a few moments, then said goodbye. I concluded my search, bending down to place the books back on the desk.

The doorknob turned. I stood up abruptly, my hair

suddenly on end. Was it the janitor? Edwina's teaching assistant? The door remained closed. The knob turned again. Knees shaking, I walked to the door and jerked it open. The hall was empty.

Was Edwina toying with me? Was she annoyed that I was sifting through her belongings?

"Edwina, are you here?"

A sound from behind me! I whipped around. The raven's eyes glinted. Had it shifted? I was sure it had been facing the desk.

"Edwina?"

The town lay sixty miles from an active fault. Had a tremor moved the statue? Yes, that was it. There had been a tremor and it had moved the raven and jostled the doorknob. I left the office, quickly locking the door.

Hurrying down the stairs, I took deep breaths of unscented air and reflected on the supernatural. In studying work of deceased poets, I often delved so deeply into meaning that I touched their spirits. C.P. Cavafy had appeared to me when I sought to identify the gender of the beloved in his poem, "Gray." Who did the gray eyes belong to? He told me not to care; it was the longing for love he wished me to remember. Years ago, I attended a séance and met the ghost of William Blake, who regaled us with tales of the devils inhabiting his drawings. Emily Dickenson, Hart Crane, and Sylvia Plath—all had communed with me on an etheric plane. I had delighted in those associations, but Edwina could be another matter and I still had a bruise on my wrist from that slap at the graveyard.

In the main entrance, a lone student leaned against the wall, looking at his I-phone. I asked if he'd felt a tremor and he said no.

Edwina had moved the raven. Was she trying to tell me

she was pleased I'd agreed to write her story? She had never been gracious in life, so I had trouble believing she would be so in death. No, she wanted something more.

I hurried home, eager for its security and Mathieu's warmth. By the time I turned onto my street, I had convinced myself that Edwina had no score to settle with me and so her spirit, while possibly restless, meant no harm.

I pulled into our driveway. Mathieu stood by the mailbox, talking to our auburn-haired neighbor, Sybi Olivette, an art history doctoral student. Gathered at their feet were her five cats, stretching and yawning. I thought of Circe and her drugged lions and attempted to end the comparison there, not wanting Mathieu to be her Odysseus.

Sybi had moved next door only six months ago. Our neighborhood, inhabited by academics, espoused a communal live-and-let-live philosophy. Everyone knew Sybi grew psychoactive plants. In her back yard, orange day lilies blossomed, morning glories crept along the fence, and marijuana thrived in the shrubs. She dried leaves in her attic. In late fall, guests entering her foyer achieved mild highs.

Her shrill laugh rang out in the evening quiet. I wondered which of Mathieu's stories from his native Togo he was telling. One of the felines, a tiger-stripe, wound its tail around his leg. He despised cats and tried to gently shake it off. When I opened my car door, Sybi turned and saw me.

"Maria!" she cried, "Mathieu was just telling me—"

Mathieu disengaged the cat's tail from his bare shin. "I was telling Sybi about feeding yams to Malokum."

They laughed and I laughed with them, remembering the tale of his father hurling yams at a sea god to ward off a storm. Standing near Sybi, I was forced to breathe in her bergamot-laden perfume. Liquid rut. I touched Mathieu's cheek, a territorial gesture for her to see. Then her cellphone rang and she rounded up her cats to go inside. Mathieu and I went in to prepare dinner. He had already laid the charcoal in the outside grill. I took lettuce and tomatoes from the refrigerator to make a salad. He washed his hands at the kitchen sink.

"Cats have a creepy feel," he said.

It was the perfect opening, but I was unable to discuss my brush with Edwina—possibly because of my brush with Sybi. Throughout dinner, I could not rid myself of the image of Sybi, her head thrown back, laughing at my darling's stories.

After we'd cleared away the dishes, I clung to Mathieu as we watched a film on Netflix. Then we departed to our studies for an hour or two of work, as was our custom. Hugh Bentley had emailed the contract for the biography. Printing it off for signature, I faxed it to his office. Until Mathieu called me to bed, I worked on the ode to Sasha Rice.

Already under the green top sheet, his black eyes telegraphed an erotic message. My senses replied eagerly. I moved toward him, but Sybi's youthful form slithered into my mind forcing me to hesitate. Was she the reason Mathieu was aroused? She'd been standing close to him, laughing at his jokes, enticing him with her scent. I suddenly felt inadequate. Turning toward the wall, I removed my clothing.

"What is this?" Mathieu asked.

I didn't reply.

"Tell me what's wrong."

"An abstract thought," I lied. "The Sasha ode."

"Ah."

Mathieu accepted the confusion poems created in my mind.

As I slid under the cover he held open for me, I ground against him, shy no more. We kissed deeply, but then the vigor went out of him.

He sighed. "Sorry, darling. Age, I guess..."

"You're not old."

"I peaked fifteen years ago," he said. "May I have a rain check?"

I kissed him. "Of course."

How easy to be a man. He turned over, went to sleep, and began to snore softly. Troubled by his reversal—I was loath to call it rejection—I tossed and turned. Was I losing his love? I tried to hold onto youth. Every five weeks, my colorist touched up my roots. At six-month intervals, a dermatologist injected Botox and other poisons into my face to smooth out tiny wrinkles. Though I wore size six, my body was losing its tone. I railed at myself for missing Zumba classes. Mathieu couldn't help but compare Sybi's lissome figure to my sagging body. If only a hag lived next door! I remembered Edwina in the rain. If I lived long enough, would I be dried up and alone, as she had been?

Mathieu and I had been together nine years. He'd come to the university to teach, and we met at a coffee shop off campus. He was seated at a table with his laptop, a pile of books in front of him when the stack fell over, hitting my knee as I passed. Stumbling, I landed in his lap. He was embarrassed. I was unsettled by the fall, but had lingered a moment, liking the hard feel of him and his smell of musk.

As it turned out, he'd been in the country only two months and knew no one. We began seeing each other, first for coffee and conversation, and then dating, taking in the symphony and theater. I introduced him to friends, who warmed to him, as I had done. Little by little, he introduced me to his culture, escorting me to a café that served deep-fried black-eyed peas and boiled plantain, and playing records of sensuous music made by zithers and sticks with jingling rings. Five months after meeting, we became lovers and a year later, he moved into my home. Loving him had brought passion into my life, and I thought I'd brought the same to him.

I turned over and looked at him, my eyes tracing his noble profile. Why did I doubt him? Two nights ago, we had made love, creating sacred moments, overriding his problems at work, my knot in Sasha's ode. Sybi had been in our lives then with her youthful exuberance, and while I found her annoying, I'd never seen her as a threat. Burying my face in Mathieu's shoulder, I finally found sleep.

Near dawn, I woke bathed in cold perspiration. In my dreams I'd heard footfalls, then turned to see Sybi in the doorway, the iron claw in her fist. I threw on my robe and went downstairs to sit by the window and watch the sun come up. I composed a poem that was a bit like a prayer.

Chapter III

That afternoon, I set out for Edwina's house, planning to stop by the child's grave afterward. It seemed odd that the little boy was buried on Frost property. Local people wouldn't have tried to bury anyone there, fearing consequences if Captain Frost discovered the evildoer's identity. Of course, a stranger wouldn't have known the land belonged to one of the richest men in the state.

Fleetingly, my thoughts returned to Mathieu and Sybi, but by the time I turned down the tree-lined lane leading to Edwina's two-story Victorian farmhouse, I'd convinced myself that out-of-balance hormones lay at the root of my insecurities. How silly I was. Of course, Mathieu loved me. How foolish I was to doubt him.

Though I'd attended departmental picnics at Edwina's farm, I'd never been inside her house. As I unlocked the front door, I paused to consider how her spirit might feel about another intrusion. In life, Edwina had been solitary, private.

The door creaked open and I stepped uneasily into the foyer, a drab cell with coat hooks on the wall. A brown wool sweater, its hem unraveling, drooped from a hook. The temperature was comfortable—Hugh had not turned off the furnace. I opened the drapes in the living room, sneezing as dust sifted down onto a threadbare carpet. A venomous green Victorian couch was piled high with journals and books.

Resting on a stained cushion was a half-eaten bag of potato chips.

Above the mantel, a portrait of a beautiful woman smiled down on the disorder. I gasped—it was Edwina. How lovely she'd been in her youth! What had happened to pinch those comely features into the withered crone she became in later years?

The portrait distressed me. I wandered into the dining room and drew a line with my fingertip in the table dust. Piled high on the buffet were books in opened boxes from mail-order houses: *Methods of Murder in the Seventeenth Century, Poisons from the Meadow, Executions, a History.* What was she working on before she died?

White metal cabinets and a green table with ladder-back chairs greeted me when I walked into the kitchen. The refrigerator, an old model, droned loudly. Second hands on a wall clock sounded like a tongue clucking at metered intervals. Dirty dishes were stacked in the sink. On the counter sat a plate with a rose petal design, half of a desiccated roast beef sandwich, the spiky end of a gherkin, and a wadded-up napkin.

Edwina's last meal?

I was appalled that no one had removed the plate. Although Edwina and Louise were at odds, Hugh could have seen to it. Since he was so concerned that his aunt's strangeness would taint his campaign, why hadn't he sent a cleaning crew to the house?

The refrigerator thrum got on my nerves and I left the room. The stairway was enclosed, the door shut, and I paused before opening it. As with the other doors, it rasped open. All the hinges could have used a dose of household oil. Gripping the bannister, I stepped carefully on worn stair treads, careful not to trip, and headed for the second floor.

With all the royalties Edwina had earned, why hadn't she laid new carpeting? Her house attested to miserly traits.

At the top stretched a long, dark hall. My nose picked up smells of old wood and staleness. Spider webs, dotted with husks of flies, trailed from the crown molding. I moved on. Six open doors led to four bedrooms, a study, and a storage room. More empty boxes. The upstairs seemed colder than the lower level. I wondered if the registers were closed. Possibly, Edwina liked to sleep in the cold.

The bedroom nearest the stairs revealed an unmade bed and I assumed it was where Edwina had slept. Her duvet was thick and poufy and the color of bruised cherries. The furniture was Art Deco in design, waterfall pieces with rounded edges, popular in the late 1920s and 1930s. There was nothing on the walls except a clock with Roman numerals. I smelled jasmine. The scent was so strong, I sneezed. As I wiped my nose, a sense of foreboding came over me. Edwina did not want me in her bedroom. I stepped quickly into the hall.

Certain her ghost was hovering, I glanced uneasily into her study and found it even more disordered than her office. Papers littered the floor, as if a tornadic wind had blown through the room. I longed to gather them up, to see what she was working on, but feared—

A sense of peace buoyed me up. Edwina had tacitly given permission for me to enter. Breathing more easily, I gathered up the pages, saw they were numbered, and put them in order. It seemed to be an unfinished manuscript, ending on page 73, and missing pages 1-10 and 34-48.

I sat in a rocking chair to read the draft, a story about a Jesuit priest named Father Jean-Louis, who lived near a body of water—she called it a sea, and a little later, a river. Perhaps they were two different things—the sea and the river—and he lived between them. The priest suffered severe headaches; there were several descriptions of him holding his head "between long-fingered hands" and screaming in pain. This first occurred on page 50 and recurred on pages 63, 66, and 69. Page 73 ended in mid-sentence: *The pain was sent by the—*

Had Edwina experienced debilitating headaches? Had she been so absorbed in her new creation, Father Jean-Louis, that she ignored her own warnings of stroke? The thought stunned me. Had Edwina thought she could *will* her symptoms to a character? I could see how it would happen. How many times had I wished to describe a true feeling—not a description—and forced myself into a simulated state of joy or hatred or envy—whatever it might be—so I could get the *feeling* on paper?

I began to look for the beginning and middle pages. The kidney-shaped desk with its long middle drawer and eight drawers, four to a side, beckoned me. In the lower left drawer, I found a copy of her contract with her publisher for a new book, as yet untitled. It was signed. A large blob dotted the "i" in Edwina. The mid-stroke on the "F" was a fevered slash.

The middle drawer contained the beginning of the priest's story, which started with commentary on the Society of Jesus in North America. Edwina, like Michener, often began her stories by probing deep into the aboriginal past. She dropped in the priest at the end of the second chapter. He was a tortured soul, newly arrived on the continent, terrified of Indians. He battled the sexual taunts of a settler's daughter, Brigitte, who was impossible to avoid because he served daily communion to her dying brother. Attempting to drive her from his thoughts, he tormented his body by walking barefoot on live coals and gouging his genitals with sharp sticks. Ugh! Edwina continued in that vein for another three paragraphs, but I couldn't bear to read on. Had she been punishing herself as well as the priest?

As I'd noted, pages 34-48 were missing. On page 49, Edwina wrote:

> *I will not temper my words for the sake of the faint-hearted. I began to kill. My first victim was the farmer's son. If he were dead, I would have no reason to go to the farm. I strangled the boy with my bare hands and threw him down the well. When Mademoiselle Brigitte woke to fetch the morning water, I took her to the river's edge, slit her throat, and sank her body with heavy stones.*

Why did a pious priest become a rampaging murderer? I continued my search for the missing pages, but never found them. Something significant must have been written there—perhaps they contained the key to Edwina's own discontent. Had she named Jean-Louis after her hated sister, Louise?

The door slammed shut. I jumped. Where had the blast of air come from? None of the windows were open. Had I overstayed my welcome? Hurrying downstairs, I intended to bolt for the door, but something calmed me and I paused to admire Edwina's portrait. A film was drawn over the picture like a tightly woven net; it had not been there before. I reached up to touch it, only to have it disappear.

Was Edwina displaying a playful side?

"Edwina," I said. "What a lovely likeness."

Did a sudden swoosh of air ripple the drapes? Did she mean it as acknowledgement of my compliment? Feeling on safe ground, I took a moment to study the portrait. Edwina must have been in her twenties when she sat for it. Her cheekbones were sculpted; her dark eyes showed—I fumbled for the word—and then it came to me: *experience*. Her well-proportioned frame was clothed in an ivory gown, empire-style, with a low neckline and long sleeves. A tiara of ivory roses nested in her dark hair. It could have been a bridal portrait, but I was under the impression Edwina had never married. To be sure, I needed to ask Louise. The artist had signed the painting A. Cyr. He was a local painter of some renown, who had died a few years ago. I remembered reading his obituary.

As I looked again at her eyes, wondering what secrets they held, I heard a creak from the kitchen, followed by a draft of cold air. The back door was locked. I'd noticed it as I peered out its windows. Probably field mice, I thought, creeping about for a warm place to nest. But how mice would let in a draft, I had trouble explaining. Was Edwina playing another trick? Did she want me to leave? I hesitated, then walked toward the kitchen.

"Edwina?" I called.

A chair fell, a plate crashed to the floor.

Heart racing, I entered the kitchen. A chair lay on its back. The plate was knocked to the floor and broken. The back door was shut, but the small curtain on its window moved, as if someone had just gone through the door. The disarray seemed too heavy-handed to be the work of a spirit. Had someone been watching me? I picked up the chair and stooped to pick up pieces of the broken plate. As I lifted a shard caught between the floorboards, I saw a small, wedged object.

Without thinking, I reached into drawers until my fingers gripped a knife, which I used to pry loose the object—a tiny silver spoon, badly tarnished. I thought back on the family's lineage. It might have been used to feed Louise when she was an infant. The Frosts had moved to the farm following her birth.

Not certain what to do with the spoon, I left it on the table for Hugh to find. Depositing the shards in the garbage can, I saw something I hadn't noticed earlier: a pet flap cut into the back door. Edwina had kept dogs and this was how they went in and out. Some other creature had surely discovered it and I had scared it off. Nearly satisfied with that conclusion, I hurried from the house, locking the front door behind me.

Trying to sort out which of the happenings—moving drapes, slammed doors, the commotion in the kitchen—were caused by a spirit or natural phenomena, I almost drove past the child's grave. Braking near the wooden bridge, I got out of the car. Half-sliding down the mud bank, I hung onto willows to keep from falling. The grave's location was marked with stakes. Black soil veined with clay was heaped at the side of a pit that appeared to be about four feet deep. Water had seeped into the hole.

The spot was isolated. Swollen with April rains, Sugar Creek was probably fifteen feet wide below me, before it meandered through fields and spilled into the Wabash River. Nodding cattails and weeds lined the bank. Farther back, a row of spiny hedges rose like prehistoric creatures.

Anger spiraled inside me as I gazed at the forlorn hole in the ground. The boy's remains had been cast away as if they were trash. Had he been loved in his short life? Were mourners present when he was lowered into the grave? Did anyone bless him? Or had the burying been done by strangers, quick to hide evidence of their crime?

I looked at my watch. Nearly five. Though I needed to leave, something compelled me to stay. What could I learn standing near the boy's grave? Staring into the pit that had held his body, I saw nothing but silty loam. Imaginings formed in my mind, thin prehensile tails growing from—

Not tails. Tales. The dead boy had a story and I determined to discover what it was. Was he connected to the Frosts? The newspaper reported he'd been in the ground for a half-century or more. Louise Bentley was in her seventies. Fifty years ago, she could have heard gossip about a missing boy. Returning to the car, I called Hugh, telling him I needed to speak to his mother. He gave me Louise's number and she answered on the third ring.

"Be quick," she said. "I'm going to the theater tonight."

"I'll be there in a half hour," I said.

* * *

Louise lived on the top floor of the downtown Bentley Hotel, named after her late husband's father. I went up in the elevator. She admitted me immediately, as if she'd been standing by the door. She wore a cobalt blue evening suit with a silver scarf tied artfully around her neck.

"This can't take long," she said. "I told you. I have an engagement."

As I fished in my handbag for my notebook, I noticed a wall portrait of a handsome young Marine: Stuart Bentley, Louise's older son, who had been killed in Viet Nam. I remembered Stuart from the sport pages of the local newspaper: he had been a high school basketball star. He resembled the Frosts.

Louise followed my gaze, her features softening. "Stuart was a brave soldier."

A hallowed moment. Silence followed. I lost my focus, and Louise, some of her impatience. I'd come to ask if she remembered a boy who had gone missing when she was young, but drew back. Louise had shown a tender side and I didn't want to lose an opportunity to build trust with her. Instead of my original question, I asked why Edwina had commissioned the portrait that hung in her living room.

Her response was curt. "No occasion. Edwina was very vain."

The spell was broken, so I persisted. "It looked like a bridal portrait."

"It may have looked like one, but it wasn't. Edwina never married."

"Were there men in her life?"

A shrug of cobalt shoulders. "Not that I remember."

"She was very beautiful, as a young woman."

Louise slapped her silvery gloves against her left hand. "Depends on your taste, I suppose. She had a rather long nose."

I chose my words carefully. "Your dislike for your sister is obvious. What happened between you?"

A storm brewed in her dark eyes. "Edwina and I had nothing in common. She was eight when I was born and —" She broke off sharply. "You need to go."

With nothing to lose, I blurted: "I stopped by the creek where the skeleton was found. Do you remember if a boy went missing when you were young?"

She cried out for her maid and flung herself on the sofa. The maid hurried in. Louise demanded that I leave, her voice icy with rage. And leave I did, quickly. Leaning against the elevator wall, I closed my eyes.

Louise knew who the boy was.

Retrieving my notebook, I reviewed birth dates for the Frost family. Who, besides Edwina and teen-aged Louise, were of child-bearing age fifty or sixty years ago? I ruled out their mother, who had died in 1938. James Hawthorne's mother, who was Captain Frost's sister, would have been forty. Suddenly I thought of the Frost men. Did Captain Frost, William Bentley, or James Hawthorne father the boy? I punched the button and rode down to the ground floor. I felt sick. Did I still want to tell Edwina's story?

Chapter IV

L ate April. The morning sun brought warmth. Since it was Saturday, Mathieu lazed his way through breakfast, taking his coffee to the patio where I joined him a few minutes later, bringing quiche and muffins. I'd intended to discuss what happened with Louise, but Sybi spied us from her kitchen window and invited herself over. Decked out in a V-necked, red and gold muumuu and reeking of bergamot, she brought photographs of voodoo fetishes from Benin.

I turned away as Mathieu greeted them with a whoop of glee. "Dried monkey heads!" he cried. "Where did you find these pictures, Sybi?"

She settled into a chair beside him. "In the storage room next to my office."

I fetched a cup for Sybi and filled it with coffee.

To escape her perfume, I went back to the kitchen. Through the window, I saw her bend over my lover, exposing considerable cleavage.

"Maria," called Mathieu, "Sybi would like a slice of quiche. Can you bring a plate and fork?"

I went to my study. Let *him* get her a plate and fork! In a few minutes, I heard him come in, rattle the dishes, and then go out again. Busying myself, I waited for Sybi to leave. After what seemed an interminable length of time, she must have done so. Mathieu came in, whistling, moving around the house before coming upstairs to give me a kiss. I decided to alert him to Sybi's machinations.

"Mathieu," I said, "there's something—"

"Can it wait, Maria? I'm composing a lecture on pre-colonial cultures. Sybi gave me an idea on how segue to voodoo."

I watched him close the door to his study, resenting Sybi and her dried monkey-head fetishes. Then I heard a door slam and looked out my window. A young man in a red convertible had pulled into Sybi's driveway. She flew out the door to greet him with a hug.

Sybi had a boyfriend! My body flooded with relief: I had misinterpreted her feelings for Mathieu. Thankful I hadn't raised the issue of her flirting, I keyed in my gynecologist's number and requested a prescription to calm my nerves. My anxieties had to be due to leeching hormones.

I returned to Louise's reaction to my question about the dead boy. Had her father sired a child on one of the housemaids? Fearing disclosure, had he killed it? But why wait until the child was a year old? Had the maid run away and returned with the child to demand hush money? But why kill the child and not the maid? Was another body buried near Sugar Creek?

Dark thoughts troubled my mind as I lived through the next few days. I also had to deal with side effects from the antidepressant prescribed by my gynecologist—blurred vision and dizziness—which slowed progress on the biography outline. I wasn't in a generous mood and was impatient with Mathieu. My behavior upset him and he sulked in his study at night.

Once the side effects abated, I was myself again. Mathieu and I enjoyed nights of glorious sex and drifted back into the calm sea of our relationship. Hugh's check for my advance arrived in the mail and I deposited it in my bank account, smiling at the prospect of vacationing with my love in the hills of Tuscany.

Renewing my search for the missing pages of Edwina's manuscript, I contacted her teaching assistant, a young woman with thick golden locks and pale green eyes. She met me in the faculty lounge.

"Where did Dr. Frost do her writing?" I asked, after we sat down.

"Her house, office, restaurants, the library—wherever the muse struck."

"I found her work-in-progress, but pages are missing. Do you know where they could be?"

She shrugged. "Maybe in her briefcase."

"I didn't find a briefcase in her office."

"Dr. Frost died at home. It's probably there."

I hadn't seen the briefcase in Edwina's house, but I hadn't searched for it either. The girl's mention of the library reminded me of Edwina's story about the Jesuit priest. She might have done research in the religious studies section of the university library. Heading across campus to the library, I speculated that Father Jean-Louis might be based on an actual person.

The handsome Palmer Library, like so many buildings on campus, had been endowed by the Frost and Bentley families. I climbed the broad marble staircase to the third floor, which housed the religious studies collection. The librarian, an androgynous-looking man with wire-rimmed glasses, looked up as I approached the reference desk. I knew better than to inquire if he knew Edwina, and if so, what books she'd checked out: librarians believe the privacy rights of patrons are inviolate. Instead, I asked about Jesuits in

North America on the eastern seaboard—I believed Father Jean-Louis had lived on the coast near a river. The librarian led me to an appropriate section and selected five tomes for perusal.

"These must not be used much," I said, hoping to elicit the response that an elderly woman had recently looked through the books.

"They're not," the librarian agreed. "I had to dust them off a few weeks ago when someone wanted to look through them. Can you be more specific about what you're looking for?"

"I need information on a homicidal Jesuit priest who came to the new world, probably in the seventeenth century."

He raised his eyebrows. "I'll see what I can find."

I paged through the books, looking for historical maps. When I found them, they were of little help; Eastern Canada was heavily veined with rivers. For two hours, I pored over the volumes, reading about the followers of St. Ignatius Loyola who fought Satan for the souls of North American indigenous peoples. There was nothing about an aberrant priest who turned to murder.

Unable to complete my search, the librarian took my email address and said he'd get back to me. I thanked him and left, driving to Edwina's farmhouse to find her briefcase.

* * *

A car drove up the lane as I unlocked Edwina's front door. James Hawthorne, her cousin, got out. Absent the strain of grief, he looked younger. I guessed he must have a key to the house.

"You're Maria, the poet who's writing Edwina's life story," he said. "You were at the funeral."

He smiled as he shook my hand. He could have fathered

the dead child, so I searched his face for some indication of baseness. His clear blue eyes stared back at me, guileless, or so it seemed.

"That's right," I said. "I'm looking for her briefcase. She was working on a book when she died and the manuscript has missing pages. I'm trying to find them."

Was it purely coincidence that he'd driven up behind me? I still felt uneasy about the incident in the kitchen. Though I'd blamed a wild animal that might have come in through the pet flap, I had felt something there—a presence. Had it been James? Had he been hiding? Perhaps in the basement? Was there something in the house he hadn't wanted me to find?

"Have you looked in the basement?" he asked. "That's where Edwina usually wrote."

I hadn't thought to search the basement.

Saying he'd stopped by to pick up books he'd loaned his cousin—an excuse that seemed plausible—he led me through the kitchen to an enclosed back porch. It crossed my mind that if James Hawthorne had been responsible for throwing the chair and plate on the floor, I might not want to accompany him to the basement. But didn't he resemble Pär Lagerkvist, the Swedish poet whose work I loved? I looked at him again and decided to trust him.

He switched on the light at the basement door and we went down the wooden stairs. The living area was paneled in oak. Near the ceiling were two rectangular windows curtained in blue and gray striped muslin. A bank of file cabinets flanked one wall, and positioned between the windows were a metal desk and chair.

"She liked to work down here," James said. "Enclosure stimulated her imagination." He pointed to the desk. "That's where she died."

Beside the desk lay a brown shoe, an oxford style with laces. In her death throes, had she kicked off a shoe?

"Where...where is her other shoe?" I asked falteringly.

"Must've come off in the ambulance. They tried to revive her. It was too late." He picked up the shoe and placed it on top of a cabinet.

It distressed me to think of Edwina dying alone in a dark, underground place, surrounded by file cabinets. There was no telephone on the desk. I didn't think she had a cellphone.

"Who found her?" I asked.

"I did. When she got up that morning, her tire was flat and she called me to change it. If I'd come right away, I might have saved her, but I didn't get here until after two."

He moved to the desk, opening and closing drawers. Finally, he stooped to look into the kneehole.

"Aha!" he said, retrieving a worn leather briefcase with ink smudges, and handing it to me. I sat on a metal chair and opened it. Inside were the missing pages. I was tempted to read them, but James Hawthorne's presence afforded another opportunity.

"James, if you don't mind, I'd like to ask you a few questions about Edwina."

He looked at his watch. "It's nearly dinner time and I'm hungry. Why don't you follow me to the Zuider Zee Café in West Oak. We can talk there."

I called Mathieu, leaving a message that I wouldn't be home for dinner, and followed James to West Oak, a hamlet of 1,500, according to a roadside sign. He stopped in front of a structure styled like a Dutch windmill, whose sign read Zuider Zee Café.

In my glove compartment, I had stowed a tape recorder, hoping to use it for interviews, and I shoved it into my purse. We went inside the cafe, found a table, and read the menu.

A petite waitress in a blue dress and white apron approached. About my age, she had short red hair, peach-toned skin, a small pink mouth.

"Mr. Hawthorne," she said with a quick smile. "It's nice to see you again."

James smiled. "Hello, Irene. How have you been?"

"Just fine." She sent him a somber look. "I was sorry to hear about Dr. Frost."

"Thank you."

"She came in sometimes with you, I remember."

"That's right. She was fond of your potato soup."

Irene took a green pad from her apron pocket and wrote down our orders. After she left, James said Irene's great-aunt had worked as a nanny for the Frost family.

"What was her name?" I asked quickly.

"Annie, I believe. Annie Henderson. She died a few years ago."

Too bad, I thought. Annie Henderson surely took useful information to her grave.

Placing the tape recorder on the table, I asked, "Do you mind if I tape our conversation?"

"I suppose not. I don't have anything to say that's not for publication."

I smiled. His blue eyes reminded me of Nordic rivers and I wondered how he had fared with the ladies fifty years ago.

"You were Edwina's first cousin," I said. "Were you close?"

"I edited her manuscripts before she sent them to her agent." He paused as Irene placed two iced teas on the table. "I own a bookstore in Otterbein, and am somewhat of an expert on Poe."

"His poetry?"

James Hawthorne contemplated the ceiling, then recited:

"Fair isle, that from the fairest of all flowers
Thy gentlest of all gentle names dost take!
How many memories of what radiant hours
At sight of thee and thine at once awake!"

I identified the poem: "'To Zante.' The hyacinthine isle."

Having established a kind of camaraderie, we looked pleased with ourselves and each other. He loved poetry. I no longer thought him capable of menacing me or ransacking Edwina's kitchen.

He sipped his tea. "As a boy, I became interested in poetry. Poe was my favorite."

I spread my napkin on my lap as our food arrived. "How fortunate for Edwina that you shared her interest in literature. What can you tell me about her early life? I know she was born in Chicago."

He lifted his fork. "Edwina lived a privileged childhood, first in a forty-room mansion in Lincoln Park, then in the farmhouse. There was another structure on the farm—Captain Frost called it a barn—that was used for lodging for the staff. Edwina had her own study there, where she could be assured of quiet. After the captain's death, the building fell into disrepair, and Edwina and Louise agreed to tear it down."

"So they've not always been in disagreement?" I asked quickly.

"It benefitted them both to raze the barn. A field was extended, meaning larger crop yields and greater profits."

"Why did they fall out in the first place?"

"It had to do with selling the land. Edwina didn't want to sell and Louise did. Eventually, they worked out an arrangement where Louise sold her half. Edwina kept hers and continued to live in the house."

"It was common knowledge they quarreled over the land. Everyone saw the photo in the newspaper—"

His eyes became glacial. "The photographer should have been fired. It wasn't Edwina's finest moment."

Hastily, I shifted to another topic. "Edwina was attractive when young. Louise said she never married. Was she ever romantically involved with anyone?"

Did he tense at the question?

"I'm certain there must have been a man or two who caught her eye, but she was dedicated to writing."

"Was her portrait done for a special occasion?"

He slid his eyes at me. "It was a whim, I think. If I recall correctly, she had just finished *The Bride of Guernsey*."

The Bride of Guernsey was a Bluebeard tale about a wife who survived a faithless, villainous spouse.

"Did she see herself as the protagonist?"

"She might have fantasized about being a bride," he said smoothly. "Wouldn't most women in that day?"

Edwina was not like most women of the 1950s. James knew that and so did I. She was pursuing an academic career and though she had yet to publish her horror fiction, the savage stories were swirling in her mind. Then I wondered if she had fallen in love with a man, only to be disappointed. The gentleman might have intuited her alter ego and found it repugnant.

I switched to Edwina's childhood. "Her stories were so dark. Was her childhood especially unhappy?"

He frowned, thinking it over. "I don't think it was in Edwina's nature to be happy. She was a solitary child. Bookish."

"Did she play with other children?"

"I'm Louise's age. Edwina was at least twelve before I even noticed her. I have no idea who her friends were. She and

LYNNE HANDY

Louise were homeschooled. She probably played with the
neighbor children. The Alsops down the road had children
her age." He paused. "You need to understand that Edwina
was sensitive, though she didn't let the world see that. I don't
think she ever got over her mother's death. She was nine
when it happened."

I consulted my notes. "Was her mother's death an
accident?"

"Louise's birth was difficult. My aunt never recovered.
Heart disease took her, I think."

We sat in silence for a few moments. I made a show of
turning off the tape recorder, then asked the question that
had devastated Louise Bentley.

"Is there any connection between the Frost family and the
child's skeleton found by the bridge?"

He fixed me with a scathing look. "I don't know why you
would ask that. Of course, there's no connection."

"I thought perhaps a servant girl might have—"

"No! Nothing like that! You've overstepped, Professor Pell."

Overstepped: to go beyond the means of taste.

"Terribly sorry," I said.

But I wasn't sorry. Someone had killed a helpless child
and buried him beside a creek. We finished our meal with
scattered chit-chat about Amy Lowell and parted with chilled
good-byes.

On my way home, I wondered at the memories my
questions had stirred in James Hawthorne. He, too, knew
something about the dead child.

I considered Edwina's childhood. Had she grieved all her
life for her mother? At age nine, she would be approaching
adolescence with no mother for guidance. A difficult
situation. I thought of the photograph with Captain Frost's
weighty hands on her shoulders. Involuntarily, I shivered.

To my great annoyance, I found Mathieu in the living room, entertaining Sybi Olivette and the young man I'd seen in her embrace. Disappointingly, he turned out to be her brother. Mathieu fixed me a martini and I was forced to join them. Contrasting my simple black tunic, leggings, and flats, Sybi wore a short, flouncy skirt and six-inch platform soles. When she stood, she was taller than Mathieu.

Did I see Sybi slide her hand down Mathieu's thigh? I wasn't sure.

The Olivettes stayed until midnight.

"Interesting young woman," Mathieu said, after they finally departed.

I kept my tone casual. "Doesn't she have a boyfriend?"

"Not that I know of."

I let the touching incident go. I might have been imagining things...

As I carried a tray of glasses to the kitchen, I glanced at the newspaper Mathieu had spread on top of the kitchen island. Another article about the dead child. An antique toy collector had identified the metal truck found in the toolbox as a GMC model produced by the Moline Pressed Steel Company in Georgia in the late 1940s or early 1950s. The truck had been expensive at the time. It seemed reasonable to conclude the child belonged to a family with means.

"Are you reading about the truck?" asked Mathieu.

"Yes." My voice sounded hoarse.

Mathieu threw up his hands. "Why did no one report the boy missing? A child has family—parents, aunts, uncles, grandparents!"

I cast about for answers that did not involve Edwina and her family. "Perhaps he belonged to people who were transitioning, leaving behind their extended family."

The words sounded hollow. Why did I say them?

"Yes, that could be," said Mathieu, staring hard at me, "but I don't think so. People with money cover things up."

I was thinking the same thing.

Chapter V

I read the pages found in Edwina's briefcase. From the arc of the story, I estimated she'd planned the novel to be at least three hundred pages long. The pages carried Father Jean-Louis through his first murders. His victims were fur traders, Indians, and French settlers.

The manuscript provided scant insight into why the priest became homicidal, except for an allusion to an act he'd committed before reaching the age of reason, which according to Roman Catholic doctrine, was seven years. Had Edwina committed an abhorrent act before her eighth birthday? Louise was born when she was eight. My imagination ran wild: did Edwina have something to do with her mother's death?

But Isabel Frost had died when Edwina was nine—two years past the age of reason. If she committed murder then, she would be guilty of sin.

There was a cryptic line in the text saying when Father Jean-Louis was born, he was the child *who was not meant to be*. Edwina used the phrase three times. She also dropped a subtle clue that the priest might be a woman:

Jean-Louis had unusually small feet with long shins.

Where Edwina was going with the story, I couldn't tell.

Was it a tale of sin and redemption? How was someone redeemed after committing mass murder?

After listening to the tape of my interview with James Hawthorne, I assembled a chronology of Edwina's life and discovered a gap. Her college years, employment, and early awards were accounted for, as were events in later life, but the mid-1950s, when she was in her twenties, were blank. She didn't seem to have been teaching or writing. Was she working on her dissertation? I checked. She'd earned it in 1953. Thinking her agent, Leslie Hirsch, might know what she'd been doing, I called his office and set up an appointment for a Skype interview the following week.

Hugh Bentley's concern that someone might dig up dirt on his aunt nagged at me, so I called him to ask what he meant.

He exhaled. "Maria, when one is related to the Queen of Horror Fiction, isn't that a logical concern?"

Aware he had avoided answering my question, I didn't pursue it. I needed to be able to work with the family.

"Fair enough," I said, "but I need family background from you and your mother. When can we get together?"

"Have you spoken to James Hawthorne? He and Aunt Edwina were close."

"I had dinner with James a few days ago. He told me only enough to whet my curiosity."

Hugh pounced. "What did James say?"

Actually, the most productive part of my conversation with James was what he *didn't* say.

"He said she was an unhappy child," I said lamely.

"I imagine she was. She lost her mother early." He paused. "What else did he say?"

"She had admirers..."

"Did he say who they were?"

"No."

"I fail to see why you need so much information." Hugh sounded peeved. "Why can't you just write about her books?"

"To understand her work, I need to know who she was."

"But you know enough. She was an academic, a writer—"

I shifted focus. "What's the story about the dogs?"

"Dogs?"

"Didn't someone call the sheriff about Edwina's dogs?"

"I don't know. You'd need to ask Mother."

"I'd like to do that. When can we get together?"

"This afternoon," he said. "Come after lunch."

* * *

Louise looked stunning in a mauve suit and gray pumps, but her mouth was a purple slit—she hadn't wanted to come. I couldn't help but notice she had small feet and long shins like Father Jean-Louis. Had Edwina wished Louise was never born? It seemed a fair question—according to James, Louise's birth had weakened their mother's heart.

"Mother," said Hugh, "you might tell Maria about Grandmother Frost." He turned to me. "She had an interesting history. I never knew her, of course."

"Neither did I," Louise said testily. "I was a year old when she died."

"You grew up without a mother," I said sympathetically, hoping to forge a bond with Louise.

"Edwina blamed me for her death," Louise grumbled, "and never, for one instant, thought what not having a mother had done to me."

I took the tape recorder from my purse. "May I tape our discussion?"

"No," said Louise.

"Certainly," replied Hugh, at the same time.

Louise rolled her eyes.

I placed the recorder on the coffee table. We sat in Hugh's comfortable chairs and I began by asking Louise how her father related to his children.

She folded her hands over the soft wool of her skirt. "He was never home. He was either in Chicago or traveling around the world."

"Who looked after you?"

"Nannies, tutors. Father hired most of them an agency in Chicago. They'd be with us for a time and then leave, only to be replaced by different women in blue uniforms. They were interchangeable." She raised a small, long-fingered hand in dismissal.

"There were eight years between you and Edwina. Did you spend much time together?"

"We took our meals together. It was Father's rule—not our choice. Particularly, not Edwina's choice."

"James said one of the nannies was a local woman named Annie Henderson."

"Yes, that sounds right," said Louise. "She's the only one of the help who didn't live in the barn."

"It wasn't an animal barn," Hugh said quickly. "It was a separate house." He went to a cabinet and opened a drawer. "Here are pictures."

James Hawthorne had mentioned the separate structure on the property. I took the photos from Hugh. The house had been shaped like a barn, painted red, with a four-angled gambrel roof.

"The Captain needed more space," explained Hugh. "He couldn't add onto the house without cutting down shade trees and thought putting up another house would destroy the aesthetic, so he built a house with a barn's exterior."

"There were two barns," offered Louise. "One for animals

and one for the help."

"Didn't Aunt Edwina have a writing room in the barn?" asked Hugh.

Louise nodded. "Father gave her a room there, away from the noise of the house." She lifted her left hand to examine the mauve polish on her nails. "I wasn't allowed in it, although once, when Edwina was away at the dentist's, I sneaked in the barn and up the stairs. Her room was in total disarray—books on the floor, papers scattered. I looked at what she'd been writing. It was a story about a princess who'd been born without legs and had to be wheeled around in a wire contraption, rather like a cage."

Vintage Edwina.

"There was also a picture on the wall of a crudely drawn baby with a noose around its neck—I supposed it was me."

My mind darted to Father Jean-Louis and the sinful act he'd committed before the age of moral responsibility. Had Isabel Frost delivered any babies during the eight years between Edwina's and Louise's births? Had Edwina killed them? If so, why hadn't she killed Louise?

"Do you know if your mother had any live births besides you and Edwina?" I asked slowly. "Babies that might have died—"

"There may have been miscarriages," Louise answered. "Father never mentioned other children."

I hated to think the child Edwina was responsible for her mother's miscarriages. Still, there was that reference to Father Jean-Louis committing reprehensible acts as a child. If Edwina had modeled the priest on herself—

I moved on. "Which bedroom was yours, Louise?"

"My room was in what became Edwina's study. It has an eastern exposure. I like sunrises."

Recalling Edwina's bedroom with the Art Deco furniture, I

said, "Edwina had the same bedroom—from childhood to old age?"

Shaking her head, Louise fussed with the buttons on her sleeve.

"Can you imagine?" Hugh broke in. "She left it occasionally. She traveled extensively. There were several trips to Europe and Asia."

"My sister was drawn to cemeteries all over the world," said Louise. "Chinese necropolises. Roman ossuaries. Hanging coffins in Singapore. Irish druid mounds. According to her, graveyards spurred her creative force."

I envisioned Edwina tromping through tombs, her eyes lit up with excitement, as she conjured up characters and plots.

"Did she travel alone?" I asked.

"Unless the trips were university-sponsored," said Hugh. "She was a loner."

I nodded, remembering Edwina at the university union cafeteria. She always sat alone, a book propped in front of her.

"Did your nannies stay in the house so you weren't alone at night?"

"Someone slept there in case we needed something. We never had a parental substitute, if that's what you're wondering."

"How did that feel, Louise?"

She picked at a piece of lint adhering to her jacket. "Quite natural. For Edwina, it might have been different—she had known our mother." She stared out the window. "I asked many questions about Mother, but Edwina was unwilling to share her memories."

"That must have hurt," I said.

Louise didn't answer.

Hugh jumped in. "Let's talk for a moment about

Grandmother Frost. Her name was Isabel Lyons before she married the captain. She was an heir to a South African shipping fortune. Unfortunately, we have few photos of her. Aunt Edwina told me she was inclined to infirmity and refused to pose. Grandmother suffered from depression."

Hugh's recollections added to the general malaise that must have surrounded the sisters' childhood. We sat silent for a moment, and then I impulsively asked Hugh to sum up his impression of his aunt in three words.

"Angry, unhappy, and—"

"Vengeful," snapped Louise.

He looked at her. "I was about to say *distant.*"

I turned to Louise. "Why do you say she was vengeful?"

She stood, her eyes smarting with tears. "That's enough. I'm going home."

Hugh followed his mother out of the room. They lingered in the corridor, speaking in hushed voices. I turned off the tape recorder and put it in my purse.

He came back in the room and closed the door. "This is hard on Mother. If you'd just concentrate on Aunt Edwina's novels and leave the rest of it alone—"

"Hugh, how Edwina lived her life has bearing on her writing. If I don't tell that story, someone else will."

"I suppose..."

"What was your relationship with her?"

"Growing up, I wasn't around her much because she and my mother didn't get along. When Mother and James decided to sell their interest in the land—that's when I saw Edwina in full gear. She tried every legal way to block the sale."

"Wait a moment. James Hawthorne was an heir?"

"My grandfather left nine acres to James. The rest of the land was divided equally between the sisters. For tax purposes, Edwina, Mother, and James formed a corporation.

Edwina was the director. To sell their shares of the land, James and Mother were forced to vote her out as director and Mother in. Aunt Edwina was furious."

"Who is Edwina's heir?" I asked.

"The university."

"Is there a lot of money?"

"The university will get about fifty million."

Edwina had sat on a fortune. I thought of the worn carpeting in her house, her dated wardrobe. She had lived like a miser.

"Is there anything else?" Hugh had remained standing. My time with him was over.

I stood. "Yes, one more thing. About the child's skeleton, the newspaper said the reporter talked to you."

He winced. "They were bound to, because it was found on Aunt Edwina's land. Some vagrants killed a kid and buried the body by the creek. It has nothing to do with my family."

"You read about the antique collector identifying the expensive toy truck?"

"It was probably stolen." He shrugged. "Anyone capable of burying a child by the side of the road is capable of stealing a toy."

I searched his face. He seemed truthful, but he was also a politician.

He took my hands in his. "Maria, you must leave the buried child alone. It has nothing to do with Aunt Edwina, and if you go around trying to sniff out a link between him and the Frosts, people will talk. There's nothing to connect our family with this unfortunate boy, but people will assume there is and that won't be good for my campaign."

I understood. His political aspirations were at stake. Before leaving, I asked to use the powder room. Upon returning, I lost my bearings and found myself in a small anteroom dominated by a large portrait of Hugh's late father, William Bentley. I took a moment to study the man, a member of a prominent banking family. He had the bearing of a man who had lived a life of entitlement, but there was something about his eyes. A roguish cast. Why wasn't the portrait hanging in Hugh's office where people could see it?

Hugh came up behind me. "That's my father. Mother gave me the portrait when she sold the house."

"You look like him."

"I suppose so." He seemed to force a smile. "Now, let me show you the way to the elevator. You took a left turn when you needed to make a right."

We said our goodbyes and I left his building. His lack of enthusiasm for his father piqued my curiosity and as I climbed in my car, I puzzled over the Frost-Bentleys, with their veiled animosities and images of departed loved ones hung on obscure walls where few people could see them. Stuart's portrait, hanging on his mother's wall, made sense, but Edwina's, entombed in her farmhouse, and William Bentley's, relegated to an anteroom...

The Frost-Bentleys craved privacy for their sorrows. And I was sure, also guarded their secrets.

When I returned home, I had a voicemail. The religious studies librarian had found nothing about a homicidal Jesuit priest. Edwina seemingly created Father Jean-Louis out of whole cloth.

I opened my notebook, found the nascent poem I'd jotted down at Edwina's burial, and added a few words:

Through mists of time, the dead speak
in unison through unheard voices,
It is a cacophony of silence dinning.
And what about the boy, the boy, the boy?

That night, the telephone rang. Mathieu slept soundly, so didn't hear it ring. I reached for the phone.

"Yes?" I said, sleepily.

"Maria Pell?"

"Yes."

A muffled voice. Was it James Hawthorne? Was he drunk?

"Leave Edwina alone."

"Who is this?" I demanded.

Mathieu woke up. "What's going on?"

"Who is this?" I asked again.

Mathieu grabbed the phone. "Hello?" he barked, then looked at me. "The line went dead."

"A wrong number," I said.

If I said I'd been warned away from the biography, he would insist I give it up.

He pulled me next to him and fell asleep. I lay awake in the dark. Had it been a drunken James Hawthorne on the phone?

Or someone else?

Chapter VI

Casting aside the biography, I concentrated on my classes as the semester came to an end. Afterward, Mathieu and I flew to New York City to take in a few off-Broadway plays. He had my full attention; not once did I mention Edwina's name, although I could not entirely rid my mind of her and of the child found in the lonely grave. I tried to forget about the anonymous call in the night and kept from Mathieu my suspicion that Edwina's ghost was lingering on earth. He taught of his culture's obsession with voodoo with seeming detachment, but was actually uneasy with the notion of spirits. I ignored the stray drifts of jasmine I smelled as we strolled in Central Park, or sat in cafes. Edwina's spirit felt distant and I had no wish to bring her closer.

At home again, I sat in front of my computer, the Skype camera activated, and watched as Edwina's agent, a balding man with a round face, settled in front of his camera. Leslie Hirsch had been with Edwina nearly thirty years, which meant he'd agented her most successful books.

He greeted me amiably. "Hello, Professor Pell. How are you today?"

"I'm fine, Mr. Hirsch. So glad you could talk to me this morning."

"Edwina is a scrumptious choice for a biography," he said, riveting me with his eyes. "There was such a duality to her."

"Duality?"

"Her moods. In my dealings with her, she was often curt. She was tough in contract negotiations, often unreasonable. But when a story idea lit in her brain, she was giddy with delight."

Giddy? It was hard to think of Edwina as giddy.

"What did you think of her writing?" I asked.

"She had a tendency to overwrite and we argued over her constant use of metaphor, though she came to be known for her more arresting ones. Thirty years ago, readers enjoyed flowery writing, but now people have short attention spans and want action. She had difficulty making that transition."

"You said Edwina was a *scrumptious* choice for a biography," I said. "What did you mean?"

"Her private life, of course. Edwina liked men. Women too."

Edwina was bisexual? A memory of a faculty tea flashed into my mind. Edwina had sat in a corner deeply engaged with a visiting female lecturer, rumored to be gay. They had left the room at the same time and later, I heard they went to Italy together.

"I suppose she was discreet in the hinterlands," Hirsch went on, "but she had an unconventional side, which she tapped into when she came to the city. She liked masquerading as a troubadour. Edwina had a rather decent voice."

He regaled me with stories of her performances in tiny clubs where she'd sung Bob Dylan's songs and recited Ginsberg's poetry, always in some kind of costume—deerskin sheaths, daisy coronets, beaded moccasins or tights, her flat derriere covered with flowing poet shirts.

"She tried LSD, but only once," he said, "because she had a bad trip."

I listened, fascinated, as he revealed facets of Edwina I hadn't known. I first met her when I was a college sophomore. She had been a visiting lecturer. Her demeanor was reserved and her reputation unimpeachable—except, of course, for rumored dark moods, understood as forgivable extensions of the horror genre she'd chosen.

"Tell me about her lovers."

"Her affairs all ended unsatisfactorily. She was terribly jealous. If her lover so much as looked at another woman—or man—there was trouble. She drove most of her lovers away."

"Do you remember who she was involved with?"

He mentioned several deceased male authors and one female poet, Ana Valencia, who had been a contemporary of Federico García Lorca. I had not known of Valencia's association with Edwina.

"Edwina was forever trying to run away from something," he said. "If you're familiar with her books, you know the protagonist is always running away."

"What do you think she was running from?"

"Maybe that sister of hers."

"What happened between them?"

"No idea. It was longstanding, whatever it was."

"Whatever it was," I repeated hopelessly.

Leslie Hirsch smiled. "That's about all I can tell you about Edwina."

Our interview was at an end. "You've been quite helpful," I told him. "Thanks so much for your time."

I disconnected Skype, and sat for several minutes, staring out the window at two chipmunks cavorting on the lawn. Then I got to work. Googling *Ana Valencia,* I learned she resided in Málaga, on the southern coast of Spain. The year-old article stated that she suffered from Alzheimer's and lived at St. Mary's Hospital. Early photos of Valencia revealed a beautiful gypsy-like woman with wild black hair, flashing eyes, and a small, curvaceous figure. A 1970 article mentioned a get-together with our nonagenarian birthday honoree, Sasha Rice, who had been born in Spain—a fact I'd forgotten. This led me to remember that my ode was due, so I printed it off and took it to the dean's office.

As it turned out, Sasha and her granddaughter were taking tea with the dean. From the high window, rays of sunlight settled starkly on the old poet's bony form. Her white hair was wispy on her pink skull. Her watery hazel eyes blinked at motes that twinkled in the air. The dean, a fleshy woman in a granite grey suit, announced my presence and Sasha turned vaguely in my direction.

"Maria is writing Edwina's biography," the dean told her, raising her voice—Sasha was hard of hearing.

Sasha smiled sweetly. I wondered if she remembered what a biography was.

"You must find Ana and talk to her," she said in a near-whisper.

"Do you mean Ana Valencia?" I asked quickly.

"Ana..." she murmured. She fumbled for her tea cup. Both the dean and the granddaughter leaned in to save her from disaster. In the confusion, I was forgotten, so I placed the ode on the dean's desk, bade them farewell, and took my leave. As I went down the steps, I wondered how I could rearrange my schedule so I could fly to Spain and talk to Valencia.

I met Mathieu for lunch at a Kenyan restaurant. We ordered goat samosas, small triangular pockets of dough, fried golden brown. He sprinkled lime juice on his food, and I followed suit, telling him about my conversation with Leslie Hirsch. We discussed dessert and had just turned our heads to look at the blackboard menu when Sybi came in, dressed in a sarong patterned with large orange flowers and chartreuse leaves. I tensed. She rushed over and sat down next to Mathieu.

"Hi, guys. I hoped I'd catch you here." She swept us with a broad smile.

I could count every tooth in her head. Clenching my jaw, I felt the onset of a brutal headache. "How did you know we'd be here?" I asked, trying for a civil tone.

"I ran into Mathieu in the library this morning and he told me." Digging into her woven handbag, she brought out a small terracotta snail. "I bought this at the open market in town. Isn't it cute?"

Mathieu took the snail in his large hand and examined it, commenting on the detail work. Sybi leaned against him to point out eye spots on the ends of the delicate tentacles. Her hair brushed his face. My head throbbed. And Mathieu? He seemed absorbed in the snail, tracing the curve of the shell with his index finger. Sybi slid her eyes at me.

I smelled jasmine. Odd—didn't Sybi wear bergamot? Sybi leaned closer to Mathieu, her breasts brushing his arm. The room went black.

* * *

I had fainted. When I regained consciousness, Mathieu was supporting my body and fanning my face with a pamphlet advertising a kamba band. Sybi leaned over me, a pseudo-concerned expression on her face.

"Maria," Matthew said, "what happened, my darling? Another hot flash?"

His reference to menopause galled me, especially with Sybi looking on. I shook my head, struggled to sit up.

"I will take you home," he said.

"I'm headed that way," said Sybi. "I can take her."

"I'm fine," I said, reaching for my water glass.

"We insist," said Mathieu. "Sybi will take you home."

We? When did Mathieu and Sybi become *we*?

I got to my feet and lurched from the restaurant.

He grabbed my arm. "Maria, you're not well."

I tried to shake him off, but he held on until we reached the quad. Sybi tagged along. Feeling nauseated, I sat down heavily on a bench.

"Please leave us, Sybi," I gasped. "I need to speak to Mathieu alone."

She shot me a resentful look, but turned and left.

"What is it, Maria?" Mathieu's tone was patient, solicitous.

"Did you invite Sybi to lunch today?" I asked.

"I mentioned we were eating here. I don't recall asking her to join us."

"She's always barging into our lives."

"She's lonely."

I raked his face with my eyes. He didn't know Sybi wanted him. My rage drained away.

"Be fair, Maria. You've never had to break into a new community. When I arrived here, I felt isolated. My family was in Africa and I knew no one."

Mathieu was a compassionate man. Perhaps I was overreacting and Sybi Olivette was not trying to lure him away. Still—

Mathieu frowned. "Are you worried that I will leave you? For Sybi?"

I turned my head.

"You *are* worried." He knelt in front of me. "I *adore* you, Maria. You are my sun and moon. How could I leave my little poet?"

I wanted to believe him. But what if desire for Sybi lay

THE UNTOLD STORY OF EDWINA

repressed in his brain, awaiting a touch, the right words?

"I'm not attracted to Sybi. Not in the least. She is too—too American. She's too loud, she moves too fast, she has nothing to say."

Listening to him recite a string of Sybi's traits, I felt myself relax. Yes, she was all those things he deplored. I begged his forgiveness. He kissed my cheeks, my nose, my mouth. As we drove home, I realized I'd overreacted to Sybi's flirting. Was it hormones? Or was it something else? If Sybi was wearing her customary bergamot, Edwina's jasmine had overpowered it. Edwina's ghost was interfering in my personal life.

According to her agent, she'd been a jealous woman. It terrified me to think I might be soaking up the negative aspects of her persona. Was she seizing me? How could I protect myself?

Chapter VII

After Mathieu left to teach his class, I shook off my doubts, confident I was strong enough to deal with Edwina's ghost. After all, hadn't I once communed with the spirit of Dylan Thomas? What a ride that had been! When we discussed the "sensual heart," he had sought to demonstrate its location by lifting my left breast. Yes, after dealing with Dylan's ghost, I could handle Edwina!

Turning on the computer, I looked at my notes and wrote the first line of her biography:

> *Nineteen-twenty-nine was the year the Roaring Twenties ended, the stock market crashed, Picasso painted Nude in an Armchair, and Babe Ruth hit his 500th home run. Julia Peterkin's Scarlet Sister Mary won the Pulitzer Prize and Stalin sent Trotsky into exile. This was the world into which Edwina Frost was born.*

As I recorded statistics of Edwina's birth and early life, I realized my prose still sounded ungrounded. I needed more childhood details. Seemingly, the only persons who could bear testimony to Edwina's early years were Louise Bentley and James Hawthorne, but both were tight-lipped. I hadn't interviewed the Frost neighbors. Were Edwina's playmates were still living nearby? I called Hugh to find out their names.

He was resistant. I'd learned to expect nothing else from the Bentleys.

"Anyone who knew Aunt Edwina is probably dead," he said.

"James Hawthorne suggested I might want to talk to the Alsop family."

"What do you want to ask them?"

Hugh's concern for what people might say no longer amused me.

"I'd like to know if they played with Edwina when they were children," I said stiffly.

He relented. "I guess it wouldn't hurt to talk to the Alsops. Their farmhouse is north of Edwina's. The Flemings live south. I think Verity Fleming is still living. It won't do any good to speak with the people west of the farm. They moved up from Covington a few years ago and never knew my aunt as a child."

I thanked him, left a note for Mathieu, and headed for the country. The Fleming farmstead consisted of a humble four-by-four house with a barn, silo, and toolshed. As I parked in the barn lot, I saw a gray-haired woman bent over a hosta bed, pulling out dried scapes. She straightened and rubbed her back as I approached. I identified myself, saying Hugh and Louise Bentley had hired me to write Edwina Frost's biography.

She squinted into the sun. "You're from the university?"

"Yes, I teach poetry."

"I'm Verity. Verity Fleming. Let's go inside for a cup of coffee."

Her kitchen walls were papered with apples, oranges, and pears tumbling like gymnasts on a milk-white mat. We sat at a round wooden table with a centerpiece of marigolds in a red vase. Verity poured two cups of coffee from a percolator coffee pot. I didn't ask to use the tape recorder—it seemed out of place in the 1940s kitchen. I placed my notebook on the table.

The old woman's blue eyes appraised me. "What would you like to know?"

"Whatever you can tell me about Edwina Frost's childhood."

"I'm a little younger than her, closer to Louise's age. I used to go to the Frost farm with Mama to deliver eggs." Verity cast her eyes past me, as if to place herself in that long-ago farm-scape. "Edwina usually stayed inside. Mama always said she felt sorry for the Frost girls. No mother—just strangers to take care of them."

"Did you ever play with Edwina and Louise?"

She shook her head. "The Captain wouldn't have liked that. He wanted his girls kept separate from us folks. We weren't good enough. It was plain as that."

"Were you resentful?"

"Toward the captain. We felt sorry for the girls. Mama often wondered if they had anybody to give them a hug."

"How did James Hawthorne fit in?" I asked, thinking of the muddled midnight phone call.

"His mother was the captain's sister. The Hawthornes lived over by Otterbein. Mrs. Hawthorne always invited Edwina and Louise to her house for holiday dinners."

"Was James an only child?" I asked, hoping he had a sibling who could discuss the Frosts' childhood.

"He had a sister, but she died in her teens. Polio. Broke her mother's heart."

I wondered what Verity knew of a little boy who went missing a half century ago.

"The child's body, found by the creek," I began.

Verity's eyes widened. "Wasn't that awful! When they discovered those little bones, I wondered if one of those Chicago girls got in the family way and—"

"Did you hear that one of them became pregnant?"

"No, but folks were quiet about things then. Girls who got in trouble were thought to be bad. Nowadays—"

Verity spoke with dismay at the shift in moral values. I listened, then remembered the rumor about Edwina mistreating dogs.

"I understand there was a problem with Edwina's dogs..."

"Dode Alsop called the sheriff because they were running down to his house and getting in his garbage. I figured she got so wrapped up in writing stories she forgot to feed them."

"What happened to the dogs?"

"The county took them away. Reckon they were put to sleep or maybe someone adopted them. They were pedigreed, don't you know."

I concluded my visit with Verity Fleming and drove north to the Alsop farm. When I knocked on the door, no one answered, but a man stepped out of the barn and asked what I was selling. I told him my mission and he said his mother, Marjorie, might be able to help. She lived in a bungalow down the road.

"Are you Dode Alsop?"

He was.

"I was talking to Verity Fleming. She said you called the sheriff about Dr. Frost's dogs."

"Damned right I did. She didn't feed them and they were always coming down here to find something to eat. They were skin and bones."

I thanked the man and got back in my car. As I drove to his mother's house, I thought about Edwina, not caring for her dogs. Had they been some kind of failed experiment in a search for companionship? I rang the doorbell. An elderly woman, using a cane, came to the door. A rat terrier barked from the kitchen door where a chair had been placed on its side to bar entrance to the living room.

"I'm Marjorie Alsop and I know who you are," she said. "My son called on his cell phone. Come on in. We can talk, but I doubt I can tell you much about the Frost girls."

When I stepped inside, the dog began yapping. The woman yelled, "Quiet, Skippy!" and smacked the chair with her cane. Skippy whimpered and scampered away, toenails clicking on the linoleum.

"Sit down," she said, indicating an overstuffed chair. "What did Dode say your name was? Pell? I don't know any Pells. Are you from around here?"

I sat in an armchair, a crocheted afghan slung over its back. "I grew up south of Fennville in a little town called Frenchman's Key."

"That's where the waterfall is," she said, easing herself into a tan recliner.

"Yes, by the mill."

"Have you talked to Verity Fleming?"

I nodded.

"Like as not, Verity told you how the Frost girls were uppity and their father kept them away from us ragamuffins. I wonder, though, did she tell you they both wanted the same man?"

I edged forward on my chair. "The same man?"

"Will Bentley. Edwina had him first, but couldn't hang onto him. Rumor was he and Edwina were close to tying the knot when Louise stole him away."

A major piece of the puzzle finally fell in place. I knew why the sisters hated each other.

"Don't know any more about it than that," said Marjorie

Alsop.

She scowled at me and I thought she must want me to leave, so I got to my feet.

"Everything wasn't hunky dory at the Frost farm," she continued. "Those bones—"

I sat down again.

"One of those Chicago girls probably had a baby. It either fell and hit its head, or somebody killed it."

I couldn't hide my excitement. "Do you remember hearing of a child who went missing?"

Marjorie Alsop shook her head. "No, my memory's not the best anymore, but I'm sure if that rumor was going around, I'd remember it."

I thanked her and headed for the door.

"I always wondered…"

I turned. "Yes?"

"When I heard about that little boy, I got to thinking. That cousin—James Hawthorne—he was quite the looker. Maybe he got a girl pregnant…"

She had my full attention. "What makes you say that?"

"I remembered an incident with my sister Pauline. She was on her way back from taking Dad's lunch out to the field and took a shortcut through the Frost orchard. James Hawthorne was there. He tried to kiss her and she ran away. He was a randy one."

"Were there other incidents?"

"I never knew of any. He never bothered Pauline again. I wondered about Captain Frost and Annie Henderson, too."

"Captain Frost and one of the nannies?"

"He let Annie ride his horse."

"Really?"

"He was particular about who rode that horse."

Skippy came back to the chair wedged in the doorway and

began to whimper. Marjorie Alsop gave him a sympathetic look.

"Reckon he's hungry," she said.

I gave her my phone number, in case she remembered anything else, and took my leave. On my drive home, I felt like Lord Carnarvon must have felt when he opened the door to Tut's tomb. I had gained entrance to Edwina's sad, twisted world. She had suffered a cold, dreary childhood and then her sister stole her boyfriend, probably the closest she ever came to having someone love her.

I stored Marjorie's conjectures about James Hawthorne and Captain Frost in a corner of my mind.

Chapter VIII

I turned the wall calendar from July, with its picture of exploding fireworks, to August's depiction of sunny beaches and palm trees. When could I go to Spain and talk to Ana Valencia? I searched the calendar. Commitments I'd penned in dotted the little squares. Some weekends seemed free, but then Sybi would be at home. I didn't trust her around Mathieu.

When I wasn't teaching, I worked on the book. Edwina's spirit stayed away, and I thought she must approve of the research I was conducting on her behalf. After reading and re-reading her published work, I set about writing an opinion of her oeuvre. It was one thing to read a Frost horror novel and then go on to Isabel Allende or Donna Tartt, but reading Edwina's entire body of work, one terrifying tale after another, was a grueling experience.

In a spirit of gloom, I set about to write summaries of her themes. As her agent had indicated, she wrote about runaways. I felt the desperation of her protagonists as they fled harrowing circumstances. The bride of Guernsey ran from a loathsome husband who stalked her through misted bogs. In *The Rowboat*, a sea captain rowed away from an evil merchant's yacht and hid out among South Pacific atolls. *The Shattered Mirror* told of a woman fleeing her homicidal identical twin.

Edwina carried perversity to extremes. In *The Rowboat*, the villain chopped off an island chief's limbs, leaving him with a torso and head, to sit on a rattan throne and shriek out unintelligible commands. Other novels described rapes, mutilations, and killings in gruesome detail. Was she symbolically murdering Louise? William Bentley? Captain Frost? Herself? Her words concerning Father Jean-Louis, *who was not meant to be*, clawed deep into my consciousness. I'd thought she might have been referring to herself or to Louise, but it suddenly struck me that she might mean the child whose bones were found by the creek. I leaped up, accidentally knocking my cup to the floor. Fritzi barked, came running in. I knelt to pet her. My hands trembled as I sopped up the spilled coffee with a paper towel.

Was the child Edwina's?

* * *

Another report of the slain boy appeared in the newspaper a few days later. The metal box containing his remains was identified as a tool box manufactured in the 1950s. How long had the police kept that information from the public? What else hadn't they shared?

Without telling Mathieu—he would have tried to discourage me—I went to the police station, explained that Hugh Bentley had commissioned me to write Edwina's biography, and asked to see the toolbox. Hugh's name gave my petition weight. Not only was he influential, he had publicly shown support for the police the previous year, when a patrolman shot an unarmed burglar.

A thickset detective in a white shirt with rolled-up sleeves guided me to the evidence room. "You figure the dead boy had something to do with the Frosts?"

I'd expected the question. "Of course not," I lied, "but since the remains were found on their property, I might want to mention it in the book—perhaps as an aside about the kind of fiction she wrote."

"You mean something like Edwina Frost, horror fiction writer, had a killing field right outside her door?"

I scribbled his words in my notebook. "That's very good," I said. "I may use those very words."

The tin box was shelved between two cardboard file boxes. Pulling on plastic gloves, the detective took it down, set it on the table, and unlatched the lid. The top handle was missing, so he eased it open with both hands. Staring into the space where the child had lain, I felt unbearably sad. Of course, there was no happy place to lay a child's remains, but it clutched at my heart to think of him in a cold, metal box.

"He was in a fetal position," said the detective.

My eyes stung. A weight plummeted to my shoulder as if someone—Edwina—had rested her head there. Jasmine. The scent stung my eyes. My nose began to run. My body shook. I knew what was happening. I had taken Edwina's trembling into my bones. I was torn between compassion and an inner terror that I would be consumed by her grief. Involuntarily, my hand lifted to pass over the toolbox.

The detective spoke. "Don't touch it."

"I won't." I struggled to control my hand. How desperately it wanted to be inside the box!

"I said don't touch it." The detective closed the lid quickly and lifted the box back to the shelf.

I began to cry. "I'm sorry..."

He placed a gloved hand on my back. "When it's kids—"

"D-Do you have any clues as to who he was?" I stammered.

"No clues. Whoever buried him didn't want anyone to know who he was. He was buried naked."

I sensed the soft, warm baby flesh against my skin. The smell of him—talcum powder, warm milk, baby lotion—it was overwhelming. Tears rolled down my face. I was sure the child was closely connected to Edwina. He might well have been hers. Struggling to regain my composure, I willed Edwina away, and finally, felt the sorrow go. The weight on my shoulder lifted. She was gone. I wiped my eyes with a folded handkerchief the detective handed me. He didn't rush me. I leaned against the wall and took a deep breath.

"Thank you," I murmured. "I didn't realize I would be so affected."

"Like I said—when it's kids—"

I nodded. "Just...just one other thing. May I see the truck?"

He reached into an expanding file and retrieved it, yellow and shiny, with no scratches. If the wheels had been run over gravel, none of the stones had adhered to the tire treads. The paper had reported the child was a year old, give or take a month or two. Perhaps he wasn't walking yet, and had only run the wheels over carpeting or flooring.

"Did you find fingerprints?"

"Three sets. One was a child's. The others didn't match up with anything in our database."

"May...may I touch the truck?" I asked.

He hesitated. "I suppose it doesn't matter. You'll have to put a glove on."

I slid my right hand into the glove and took the truck from him. I'd expected the metal to be room temperature, but it was warm. Closing my eyes, I felt vibration from the little truck. It had been loved.

The detective's voice cut into the quiet. "Are you a psychic?"

"Sometimes I feel things."

"What are you feeling?"

I gave the truck to him. "Only that the boy was fond of his toy."

He returned the truck to the folder. "Little fellow had blond hair. Curly."

"You didn't release that information."

"The prosecutor thought it was too ghoulish."

"Did he withhold anything else?"

"Not that I recall."

The ordeal had drained me. I thanked the detective for his help and left the building, fairly certain the boy had been Edwina's son. Why else the tears?

Edwina was initiating contact with me, and I feared loss of control. Not only was she able to creep into me, she was able to do it with no warning. I knew I must not let her possess me.

Thoughts weighed heavily as I drove home. Parking in the driveway, I followed the sidewalk to the back yard. The garden, with its beautiful beds of irises and daisies, never failed to soothe my mind. The wildflowers Mathieu had planted were abloom, a fanciful blend of color. I sat on a lawn chair, all the loveliness surrounding me, to ponder Edwina's ability to invade my consciousness. I attempted to channel her to say I'd be of no use unless I remained independent. I had to let her know she had no right to invade my personal life. Was my sudden jealousy of Sybi Olivette masterminded by Edwina? Before becoming involved in the biography, I'd been tolerant of Sybi, sometimes—not always—finding her efforts to lure Mathieu away amusing. Was Edwina letting me know how she felt when Louise stole her fiancé?

My attempt to channel her failed. Did she hear my warning? I couldn't be sure, but gradually, my mind cleared. I cut a bouquet of golden asters for my study.

* * *

The next day, the newspaper published another article about the boy. The tile man, after digging a trench through to the creek, discovered a metal grip attached to a rotting wooden handle beneath the surface of the water. Investigating further, he found a spade lying on the creek bottom. Police speculated that whoever buried the boy had thrown the spade in the stream.

I mentioned the article to Mathieu, who sat across from me with a cup of coffee.

"Odd, that," he remarked. "Farmers in the vicinity take care of their equipment. They are like the Swiss and Germans with their neat farms."

"The theory is that the boy belonged to itinerants."

"If a workman carried the spade in his truck, he would not have thrown it away. A man values his tools."

I could not dispute Mathieu's words. No farmer, no migrant worker would throw a spade in the creek. Only someone who didn't have to worry about the cost of replacement would have done so.

* * *

Later that week, I ran to the open market for late summer tomatoes and spotted Louise there, a woven bag on one arm. Accompanying her was a bald man wearing a bright yellow bow tie. I recognized him as Henry Blum, a master gardener, who owned a seed shop. A year ago, I'd attended a gardening workshop and he'd been the main speaker. Louise was preoccupied with the chrysanthemums, examining plants in several pots, but her companion saw me and waved.

"Professor Pell, isn't it? How were your lilacs this spring?"

"I trimmed the inside branches," I told him. "The bushes bloomed beautifully."

Louise looked in my direction and forced a smile. "Hello, Maria. How's the book coming?" She explained to Blum that I was writing Edwina's biography. This was the pleasant public Louise, garnering support for her son's campaign.

"How delightful," said Blum. "Edwina's story needs to be told."

Louise took his arm and they moved on. I stood, staring at the chrysanthemums, struck by Blum's words: *Edwina's story needs to be told.* What did this man know about Edwina?

The next day, I went to his establishment, selecting two packages of iris bulbs from a bin. Blum, now in green bow tie, stood behind the cash register. We chatted about the bulbs and then I asked how well he had known Edwina.

"Years ago I did landscaping work for her," he answered. "I worked for Louise, too, when she and her husband lived in the house on Stonecrest. Edwina went to Europe for a year in the mid-1950s. I took care of her property."

My ears twitched. "She went to Europe?"

He shrugged. "Something to do with her writing, I think."

"What was Will Bentley like?"

"Not the kind to spend time jawing with the help. Never had any trouble working for him though."

I placed a twenty dollar bill on the counter.

"Do you remember the newspaper photo of Edwina punching her sister? Did you ever see them quarreling?"

He darted his eyes at the door. "I don't want to say anything that will make the Bentleys mad."

I bit my lip. "I'll not include anything that might cause trouble for you. The purpose of the book is to understand

Edwina and her writing."

"Well, then, you're right—the sisters didn't get along. They might have wanted what the other had. Louise married a rich fellow, had two nice little boys. Edwina was alone, but her books brought fame."

"Did you witness any of their...um...disagreements?"

"Mostly, they argued over little things, like how to tend their mother's grave, who would speak about Captain Frost at the Fourth of July celebration." Blum stared out the window. "When Captain Frost died, they had a knock-down-drag-out over where he'd be buried. Edwina wanted to lay him to rest beside her mother out at West Oak, but Louise wanted him buried where the rich folk were, in the Eastland Cemetery."

"Who won?"

"Louise. She had her mother's remains moved to Eastland. I planted some petunias around the grave."

"Edwina and Louise actually struck each other?"

"Saw it myself," said Blum, shaking his head. "Took place in Louise's front yard. Louise had a rake and Edwina had a hoe. They were really going after each other. Will Bentley tried to break it up and they both attacked him. Two against one, it was, for a while."

"How did it end?" I asked breathlessly.

"That cousin of theirs showed up—James Hawthorne. He grabbed Edwina and Will grabbed Louise. Will was bleeding. I don't know which of them hit him. Maybe they both did."

I paid for my bulbs and left the store, a vivid image in my mind of the two sisters whaling each other with long-handled gardening tools. In the full passion of their rage, they had *both* turned on Will Bentley. What was that about?

My next stop was the Eastland Cemetery.

As I drove through the gate, I looked for an elaborate

mausoleum, sure that a captain of industry would have been buried in nothing less. It wasn't near Edwina's grave or I would have seen it the day of the funeral.

I found it easily: a looming, marble structure with Doric columns crowned with a statue of Zeus. I got out of my car. Closer inspection revealed the name *Frost* carved onto the frieze. The closest graves were at least twenty feet away. An upright, white marble stone with an encircled cross read: 1st Lieutenant Stuart Edward Bentley, b. 1955, d. 1975. Stuart had been killed by a sniper's bullet near the end of the Vietnam War. I remembered reading his obituary in the newspaper. Nearby was a monument for William Bentley, Louise's husband. The family plot, except for Edwina.

I drove slowly through the tombstones, trying to remember the location of her grave. Finally, I found it, nearly as far away from the rest of the family as she—or Louise—could have contrived. Her small stone was covered with bird droppings. I whispered her name. Her spirit, if there, stayed silent.

My cell phone rang. Hugh. He was peeved.

"I heard you went to the police station to see the metal box. You know there's no connection between that boy and my family."

I took a deep breath. "Are you sure? Edwina's unfinished manuscript was about a priest who *was not meant to be.* She uses that phrase three times in 73 pages. Maybe she meant the child."

"That's ridiculous," Hugh said stoutly. "Aunt Edwina had no knowledge of that child. He was dug up two days *after* her death."

But the child was killed and buried *before* her death. When flustered, Hugh was sometimes illogical. How did he manage when arguing cases?

"We need to meet," he said.

"I'll be at your office in ten minutes."

When I arrived twelve minutes later, Hugh glared at me. "You have no evidence that the child was connected to my family."

What would he say if I told him Edwina's spirit was still roaming the earth? As a church-going Episcopalian, he most likely didn't believe in restless spirits.

"What if the boy was Edwina's son and someone killed it?" I asked. "That certainly would explain her sour outlook on life."

His face took on the hue of raw liver.

"I need to ask your mother if Edwina had a child."

"You can't ask Mother something like that. Anyway, she's gone to Florida to open her Venice home."

"I just saw her yesterday at the open market. She was buying chrysanthemums."

"Her plane left this morning."

"When will she be back?"

"In a few weeks, then she'll be gone again for the winter."

"It's probably not the kind of question you ask over the telephone," I said.

He squared his jaw. "Maybe you're the wrong person to write Aunt Edwina's biography."

I squared mine. "Maybe so."

"But we've told people you're writing the book."

Undoubtedly he was thinking how firing his aunt's biographer might look in the press.

"So *write* it," he said. "Stop dreaming up fiction and write her *biography!*"

His skin returned to its normal flesh tone. When I left, he was preoccupied.

So was I.

Chapter IX

W as the boy Edwina's? Determined to have a heart-to heart with her spirit, I went to her house in the country. On entering the kitchen, I saw someone had finally washed the dirty dishes. They were stacked on the drain board. James Hawthorne? The tiny silver spoon was still on the table and I wondered if it would make its way back to Louise. Another thought occurred to me: perhaps I'd drawn the wrong conclusion—it might have belonged to the dead boy.

In the basement, I pulled back the curtains to let in the sunset. As the room flooded with crimson, I sat in Edwina's chair—the chair she had died in

"Edwina, give me a sign," I said. "Was the boy yours?"

An hour passed. I waited. I crossed and uncrossed my legs. Edwina was either somewhere else in the ethers or demonstrating her independence or hiding. The room darkened and I turned on the desk lamp.

"Edwina," I said. "help me. Give me a sign about the boy."

No sound, except that of the gusting wind. An image of the tarnished spoon flashed into my mind. Would the spoon draw her to the basement? I ran up the stairs, came back with the spoon, and placed it reverently on the desk. I sat down again, my eyes on the spoon. Several minutes elapsed. I sniffed. What was that uncomfortable smell? Had a mouse died?

I got up and opened the window, feeling cool air rush inside. The sky was a black void. A storm was coming. Should I head for home? Then the scent of jasmine overpowered the smell of animal decay.

Come nearer, Edwina. We must talk.

The flowery smell intensified. I breathed it in, wanting to be one with Edwina—but on my terms.

Suddenly, my mind was frenzied with pictures of European vistas—a sun-swept coast, blue seas, towns hugging hillsides. I pictured a white stucco building with a red tile roof. Moorish. Spain. Málaga, specifically.

Edwina wanted me to speak with Ana Valencia.

I looked for the spoon. It was gone.

* * *

I thought of the Moorish structure the next day when I opened Edwina's novella, *Cauldron of Fate*, and found an airmail envelope bearing an image of the El Andaluz Hotel in Málaga. I had delayed long enough. I had to interrupt my schedule and fly to Spain. I taught on Tuesdays and Thursdays. If I left Thursday night, I'd have four days. Mathieu would be unable to go—he had a full load of classes.

He would be at home and so would Sybi. I felt a thud in the pit of my stomach.

That evening, I apprised him of my plans. How I wished I could exact from him a promise to keep the doors locked at night to keep Sybi away! I knew he would bridle at any suggestion of distrust. Then we'd quarrel. I didn't want to leave when he was angry with me.

"Will you be all right while I'm gone?" I asked quietly.

He came around the kitchen island to embrace me. "Don't

worry about me, Maria. You'll be gone only a few days. I'll be spending most of my time at the library. I haven't finished the article on voodoo."

"I'll freeze your favorite casseroles."

He kissed my ear lobe. "No need. I can cook."

I put down my dishtowel. We were on our way to the bedroom when someone banged on the door.

"Ignore whoever it is," said Mathieu, pulling me upstairs.

The banging continued. "Mathieu! I need help!"

Sybi.

Mathieu swore and went to the door.

"It's Rafi!" she cried, when he opened it. "He's climbed up the fir tree and can't get down!"

"Cursed cat," muttered Mathieu.

"Call the fire department," I suggested.

But Sybi grabbed Mathieu's hand and dragged him out the door. I was more than peeved. Stomping upstairs, I made travel arrangements and packed for my trip. He spent the evening trying to coax the cat down from the tree. My tasks completed, I took an opened can of tuna and set it on the ground. Rafi hurried down.

Mathieu had injured his back, squirming around in the tree, so spent the rest of the evening on the heating pad. I had wanted to make love before leaving the country, but he was in too much pain. Damn Sybi and her infernal cats! It nagged at me that I was leaving him alone with her, but there was no way around it. I had to talk to Ana Valencia.

* * *

Mathieu's back was still hurting the next day, so a colleague drove me to the Indianapolis airport. As soon as I was airborne, I took out my laptop, worked on the biography, and then dozed off. When I awoke, the plane was landing.

I took a cab to the El Andaluz Hotel, noting its outward appearance hadn't changed since its image was stamped on the envelope. It wasn't a five star hotel—more like the places where Mathieu and I stayed when we took occasional European trips. My room was small and charming, with orange walls and red drapes.

Edwina's novel, *Demonio*, had been situated in Spain, and though the city was unidentified, the besieged heroine, Lina, stayed for a brief time in a hotel much like the El Andaluz. Driven from her room, she hid in a cellar, adjacent to burial vaults, similar to those Poe described in *The Cask of Amontillado*. Had Edwina stayed at this hotel in the mid-1950s? Had she come to Spain to give birth? Hurrying downstairs, I spoke with the concierge, a middle-aged woman smoking a cigarillo. Red combs anchored her upswept hairdo.

"I'm writing a biography of the American writer, Edwina Frost," I explained in Spanish. "I believe she once stayed at this hotel."

The woman shook her head. "I do not remember the name."

"It was a long time ago—in the 1950s."

"Before my time." She blew out a puff of smoke.

"Perhaps you have old guest registers—"

She frowned. "They would be in the cellar."

I could scarcely conceal my excitement. Lina had hidden in a cellar to escape her pursuer. If it matched the description in *Demonio*, I'd have proof Edwina had been at the hotel. I could envision her sneaking down the cellar steps to soak up atmosphere for her story. I now had a two-fold mission: to view the cellar and to examine the registers.

"May I look through them?" I asked.

The concierge consulted another woman, who peered at me from a doorway with suspicious eyes.

"I will pay," I said, smiling.

The women nodded and we agreed on a price. The second woman led me down weeping stone steps into a brick-walled room. Rusted metal shelves held tan leather books, some vertical, some lying flat. A single bulb provided light. In *Demonio*, Edwina wrote of puncheons supporting the cellar roof, and I glimpsed a trail of short wooden posts leading down a murky corridor. Not conclusive—perhaps all cellars were similarly constructed—but I felt I was on the right track.

The woman helped me separate the guest registers from the ledgers, and we isolated those used mid-century. I worked for an hour, narrowing the volumes to the early 1950s. Paging through, I discovered Louise had checked into the El Andaluz with her husband in December of 1953. Their honeymoon? Louise was born in 1937, so she had been only sixteen at the time of her marriage.

What had Captain Frost's reaction been?

Mr. and Mrs. William Bentley had returned to the hotel on 31 May 1954. I found Louise's name again in August of the same year, but it was written in Edwina's bold hand, with a savage smear bisecting the stem of the F. The Frost sisters had stayed at the same hotel two months apart, but I was unsure of the significance. Perhaps Málaga was a vacation destination for the family.

I thanked my helper and took a taxi to St. Mary's Hospital, where Ana Valencia lived. Located near the foothills of the Montes de Málaga, the hospital's stucco walls blended into the tawny landscape. A wrought iron gate barred the entrance. Asking the cab driver to wait, I hurried to the gate and rang a silver bell. A young nun appeared. I presented an abbreviated version of my mission and asked to speak to

Senora Valencia.

"She is resting," the nun said, "but since you have come all the way from America, I will see if she is awake."

"Gracias."

The hospital interior was cool—thick walls kept out the heat. Touching my elbow, the nun guided me down a hallway flanked with dark paintings of saints. At the end, she stopped at a door, pushed it open, and motioned me in.

"Senora Valencia is not always in her right mind," the nun warned me, remaining by the door.

I turned to the Spanish poet who, according to Leslie Hirsch, had been Edwina's lover. Now shrunken, she sat in a wheel chair wearing a man's suit, resembling a self-portrait by Frida Kahlo.

"Senora Valencia," I said softly. "*Me siento honrado de concerte.*"

"You are American," she said. "It would be a treat to practice my English."

I thought my Spanish unaccented. Obviously not.

"Have you come from Edwina?"

Her old mind was still prescient.

Remembering one of Valencia's poems, I said, *"Do not grieve, for a soul has joined the starry weave of heaven."*

She clasped her thin bosom. "Edwina has passed."

The old poet grew silent and I thought she'd gone to sleep, but I was mistaken. Her lips were moving. She was praying.

Then she addressed me. *"The real sphinx is a clock."*

Lorca's poem. I quoted the next line: *"Oedipus will be born from its eye."*

She cackled. "You know Federico!"

"I teach his poetry."

"Sin is a blue tide."

I thought for a moment. "Valencia."

"*Sin is a blue tide that rides the night and sweeps the feet of...*" She frowned. "I wrote it and now do not remember the rest."

"*Peacocks*," I said.

She lit up like a child. "Of course. The gaudy, shrieking things!"

I leaned closer. "Edwina's family hired me to write her biography. You and she were close. What can you tell me about her?"

She sent me a sidelong look: "*Love is toes, fingers, ears; all parts of you, my dear.*"

Trochaic first line in trimester, second line in iambic trimester. Typical Valencia. I was unfamiliar with the verse. Had she made it up on the spot? Was she professing her love for Edwina?

Possibly.

But it also sounded like a line from a nursery rhyme. Had she written it for a child?

"Did Edwina have a son?" I asked quickly.

She brought her index finger to her lips.

"Death breaks the seal of secrets," I said.

"*Al gemir la santa niña quiebra el cristal de las copas,*" she said, then dozed off.

The line was from Lorca's "Martyrdom of St. Eulalia." *The blessed girl's moaning breaks the crystal goblets.*

The interview had obviously tired the old woman. I would need to wait until another day to question her further. The young nun opened the door and I went out.

"She enjoyed talking with you," said the nun.

In the corridor, my eyes fell on a painting of a red-robed St. Stephen, cowering as a vicious mob stoned him. "Is there a portrait of St. Eulalia?"

There was and she seemed eager to show it to me. We

turned down a hallway leading to a library and stopped in front of a painting of a golden-haired maiden with her head protruding from the end of a barrel. Knife hilts stuck out from the staves. As the barrel rolled, the blades would slash her to ribbons. What sadists the Romans were! The tableaux moved to the girl's beheading, where a white dove fluttered from her bloody neck. The nun crossed herself. I backed away.

Why on earth had Ana Valencia mentioned St. Eulalia?

"May I return tomorrow?" I asked.

The nun nodded. The taxi was waiting and I went back to the hotel. I tried to call Mathieu, but the line was busy. Opening my balcony door, I stepped out to view the city. The mountains lay easterly, and in the opposite direction, the blue sea sparkled in the sun. I sat for a while, alternately dialing Mathieu's number and planning my next move.

My theory that Edwina had come to Spain to give birth gained strength. She would have had support from her poet friend. Valencia may even have written a poem for the infant.

But why had Valencia quoted from Lorca's "Eulalia" poem when I asked about a child? Was it to express sympathy for tragedy? Or did it mean something else? At Valencia's age, her memory was bound to be confused, seething with her own verses and those of others. To my knowledge, Edwina had never named a character Eulalia, nor had she used a churn of knives as a killing instrument.

A thought struck me. Could one of the nuns be named Eulalia? I would find out tomorrow.

* * *

Down the street flashed the bright lights of a *tapas ristorante* and around eight o'clock, I went there for dinner.

A Roma dancer entertained in a ruffled red dress, and I thought of Lorca's poem of flamenco and death. Fumbling for my notebook, I jotted down a few stray words that I hoped would lead to a poem: wine, red lace, dancing shoes, cool night breezes. When I returned to the hotel, I went to bed and despite my concern about Mathieu, slept soundly.

Rising early the next morning, I tried without success to call him again, then had coffee and croissants in a nearby café. I returned to the hospital. The young nun appeared when I rang the bell.

"Does the hospital have birth records?" I asked.

"For that you need to see Sister Eulalia."

Eulalia! The Eulalia whom Valencia meant when quoting Lorca's poem! My heart leapt and I nearly ran over the young sister when she opened the gate. As before, we went down a long hall, but instead of turning left to go to Senora Valencia's room, we went right and ended up in a room of filing cabinets. Sister Eulalia, an ancient person, walked with a cane.

"I'm looking for a birth record," I told her. "A boy born to an American, Edwina Frost—probably in 1954."

Sister Eulalia limped to a back room, moving so slowly that I could hardly bear it. I listened to the clang of a dozen metal drawers opening and closing. At last, she returned, carrying two yellowed folders.

"I have two Americans with the surname Frost," she said, "but they are both named Louise. Louise Frost Bentley gave birth to a son in June, 1954, and the other Louise Frost, in August of the same year. She also had a son."

"May I see?" I asked.

She handed me the files. I opened the first folder. Louise Frost Bentley, age sixteen, had given birth to a son on June 2, 1954 and named him William after his father.

William? I'd never heard of a child named William.

The second folder was labeled *Frost, Louise,* and contained another birth certificate. This Louise also had a son. I nibbled my knuckle. It couldn't be Louise—she'd had a child only two months before. I thought of the hotel record—Edwina had registered as Louise. It had to be Edwina, again using her sister's name.

Edwina hadn't named the boy. Someone with initials, *SMC*—probably a nun—had scribbled in the name, *Joseph*. I'd heard that when a sickly newborn male was born in a Roman Catholic hospital, he was often given the name Joseph for the sake of a quick baptism. Did Edwina's child die at birth?

The line indicating the father was blank. Annie Henderson had signed after the word, *Witness*—Annie, the great-aunt of Irene, the waitress at the Zuider Zee Cafe.

"Do you have death records?" I asked.

Sister Eulalia replied that she did, and when I asked if Joseph might have died, she retraced her steps to the file cabinets. A few minutes later, she returned: there was no death record for little Joseph.

My brain buzzed like a flock of magpies. Two male babies: one named William Bentley and the other, Joseph. Did Joseph live and Edwina give him another name?

"May I have copies of the birth certificates?" I asked, keeping my voice calm.

A nun carried the folders out of the room and returned a few minutes later with my copies. I paid a small fee and asked if I could see Ana Valencia again, but the sister said the poet had had an uneasy night and was not coherent. I felt guilty, wondering if my questions had stirred memories better left forgotten. Regretfully, I said goodbye to the place that had been the source of so many answers.

Upon returning to the hotel, I tried again to reach Mathieu. The phone rang, but went to voice mail.

"Mathieu," I said, "Please call me."

I spent the rest of the day wandering the shops near the hotel, puzzling over the mystery of the two—or was it three boys—and trying to reach Mathieu. I phoned one of his friends, who hadn't seen him, but said not to worry—Mathieu could take care of himself. Why my anxiety? Sybi, of course. While I didn't think he'd run off with her, I suspected they were together. Perhaps he'd temporarily moved into her house—but no—there were her crawling cats.

Where was he?

At a small shop with a green awning over the door, I bought a gift for Mathieu, a plaster bull with a ring in its ear. Was that symbolic? Did I want Mathieu to have a ring in his ear so that I could tie him to a leash? No, of course not. What was the matter with me?

That night, I suffered a hideous nightmare: Mathieu was having sex with Sybi. I discovered them in our bedroom, in *our* bed. I heard a great pop of combustion and turned as the room burst into flames. Mathieu cried out to me, but we were separated by a wall of fire and I lost him. I awakened, panting, my heart hammering.

My room was dark, except for a triangle of light from a neighboring cantina that slid through the top of the drapes. Pain seared my chest. A heart attack? Dripping with perspiration, I paced my room until dawn. I tried Mathieu again before showering. He picked up on the first ring.

"Where have you been?" I cried. "I've been frantic."

"I've been in the stacks. You know how terrible reception is down there."

For the entire weekend? I fought to keep my voice calm. "I called you at least twenty times. Didn't you get my voice mail?"

"Who checks their voice mail on the weekend? Why didn't you text me?"

From the window, I saw long white clouds streaking over the sea. I weighed the sound of his voice, the pacing of his words. Was he telling the truth?

"Why the interrogation, Maria?"

"I've been trying to call for hours."

"Has something happened?"

I gripped the phone. "I had a nightmare."

He had heard my nightmares before. "Poor darling. Tell me."

"You were fucking Sybi. There was a fire and I had a heart attack."

"Maria." He said the word in three slow syllables, with a heavy accent on the second, as if I were a child.

I didn't respond.

"When are you coming home?" he asked.

"My flight arrives tonight around six—midnight, your time. I'll take a cab."

"I'll pick you up."

"How is your back?"

"I've recovered."

I hung up without saying I loved him. Hours later, when seated on the plane, I regretted taking my nightmare out on him.

Chapter X

Mathieu was double-parked at the airport curb. When he saw me emerge from the exit, he ran to embrace me. I jerked away from him. Was that jasmine I smelled on his collar? He grabbed my luggage and whisked me into the car. Once behind the wheel, he leaned over to kiss me. Yes, he smelled of jasmine. Edwina, having left me to my own devices in Spain, was back.

It was an unsatisfactory kiss, for my brain grew cold, even with Mathieu's warm lips on mine. Edwina had me in a vise. *Go away*, I told her. *You mustn't meddle with Mathieu.* Did I feel a thump on my shoulder? She was becoming impatient. She had sent me to Spain so I could learn about the child; now I had to—what? Save the child? Too late! Did she want his killer found—even after these many years? Did she want the boy buried in a respectable grave? Could that be what she wanted?

The air in the automobile cleared. Mathieu smelled of his signature musk. Edwina was gone.

"Did you find anything helpful in Spain?" he was asking.

Edwina had scattered my brain. I spoke haltingly, recapping my registry search at the hotel, my interview with Valencia, and the discovery of the birth records.

"In 1954, Louise had a son by her husband, William Bentley, and named him William, Jr.," I said. "Two months later, Edwina, identifying herself as Louise, had a son whom a nun named Joseph."

The automobile hummed as Mathieu steered down the highway. The blackness of night seemed welcoming. Edwina was swallowed up in the ethers.

Mathieu had a way of purring when he was thinking. "The little boy found in the tool box—was he one of those children?"

"Possibly."

"Whose child was he?"

"I'm unsure. I've never heard of William or Joseph."

I did not share my theory that the boy was Edwina's, and our conversation shifted to the mundane—his research, my travel experiences. Then we were quiet. I didn't know what was going on in Mathieu's head, but I was focusing on Irene, the waitress, whose great-aunt, Annie Henderson, was present when Edwina gave birth. Annie might have shared significant events with her family when she returned. Perhaps Irene could tell me something.

We arrived home. I went upstairs. Mathieu had not bothered to make the bed. As I untangled the sheets, a rank animal smell stung my nostrils: Sybi's bergamot perfume.

"Mathieu!" I screamed.

"Yes?" He ran in from the bathroom.

"I smell Sybi in our bed!"

He stared at me. "What?"

"Sybi. Her scent permeates the sheets."

He picked up an edge of the top sheet and smelled it. "It smells like it always does—that fabric softener the cleaning woman uses."

He handed it to me. He was right.

"You imagine things," he said.

As soon as he moved away, I smelled bergamot again.

Edwina was playing nasty tricks on me. I had been too quick to think she was gone. Was she attempting to expose Mathieu's infidelity so I'd leave him and get on with my life alone, as she had done when William Bentley jilted her? Or was Mathieu innocent and she was jealous of his love for me and determined to separate us?

Was my distrust of Mathieu based on fact or fiction?

That night, I slept wildly, suffering all kinds of nightmares about Mathieu and Sybi. Twice Mathieu pulled his pillow from my arms; in my frenzied sleep, I had dragged it from under his head. When I awakened the next morning, he had gone, and I looked contritely at his pillow. Would Mathieu interpret my pillow snatching as a subconscious wish to have him gone? Would I lose him? I didn't want to end up alone.

* * *

The summer session ended, and during the break, I turned my full attention to the biography, eager to be done with it. I concentrated on Edwina's novels and their placement in the order of her life, for her outward life had been ordered; it was her inner life, her secret life, that seemed chaotic and parent to her work.

I had not forgotten wanting to talk to Irene. I went to the Zuider Zee Café to see her, but she had gone on a two-week vacation with her family. I would have to wait.

The fall term began. I was teaching Spanish poets, which pleased me: I could spend time with Lorca. I rallied from bed on Tuesday and Thursday mornings to teach metaphor to my class.

"Lorca believed metaphors should have form, action, and unexpectedness," I told my students. "That's evident in his poetry."

Since most of the students were fluent in Spanish, we enjoyed a rigorous debate on whether those three requirements were more easily met in English or in Spanish. One student argued that the English language had twice as many words as Spanish and so there were more words to choose from. Another denounced English as "the language of geese" because of its sibilance, citing Emperor Charles V from the sixteenth century. It was an active class, filled with curious minds.

In mid-September, I called the Zuider Zee Café to see if Irene was back from vacation. She was. Her shift began at four—I would go around seven, after the dinner hour rush was over. Farm folks usually ate around six. I called Mathieu to say I'd be home late, as I had an interview to conduct for the book.

"I'll pick up Chinese for dinner," he said. "We can heat the food when you get home."

"Thank you, Mathieu," I replied. "I'll be home as soon as possible."

We were being careful of our relationship, both realizing we—or should I say I?—could torch it to ashes.

To refresh my memory of the Valencia interview, I turned on the computer, opened a file, and read my notes. I was satisfied with the old poet's observations. Though her mind had been fuzzy, her poetic form of communication seemed to confirm her veracity. Afterward, I reread chapters I'd written, editing along the way. Time flew. At seven, I transferred my file to a thumb drive and headed to West Oak and the cafe.

The wind was up, ruffling the rust-tinged leaves of oaks along the highway. After passing the Frost farm, I continued north to West Oak, and pulled into the restaurant parking lot. Inside, I found Irene talking to an older couple at a corner table. She saw me and showed me to a booth.

"I remember you," she said, curving her small mouth into a smile. "You came here with Mr. Hawthorne."

"That's right," I said. "My name is Maria Pell. I'm writing Dr. Frost's biography. May I ask you a few questions about her?"

"I just knew her as a customer..."

"Your great-aunt, Annie Henderson, worked for her. I'm interested in what she thought of her."

Irene glanced at a clock near the kitchen. "I suppose I could take a short break."

She sat down and focused her light blue eyes on me.

"How did your great-aunt feel about Edwina Frost?" I asked.

Irene took a moment to think. "Dr. Frost treated her well, as far as I know. Afterward, when Aunt Annie quit to take care of Gran—sometimes she'd send a check."

"That was generous of Dr. Frost," I said slowly, wondering if Aunt Annie had been blackmailing Edwina.

Irene must have heard the hesitation in my voice. "My aunt had worked for Dr. Frost for several years," she said spiritedly. "She was paid cash. There was no retirement fund."

The Frosts had ducked paying social security? Hugh wouldn't like that information

Since Irene was not chatty, I had to prompt. "Did your aunt tell stories about working for the Frosts?"

"Once in a while. There was the time she went to Spain. That was a big thing. No one in our family had been out of the country before. Aunt Annie and Dr. Frost sailed on a ship, and stayed in Spain for several months."

"Did she say what they did in Spain?"

"She talked about the food and the music. She liked the sea."

"Did she say anything about a baby?"

Irene blinked. "A baby?"

"About Dr. Frost having a baby."

"Dr. Frost didn't have any children." Irene looked out the window where a teen-aged boy had parked his pickup truck next to my car. "There's my son. He stops by for a sandwich after football practice."

She started to get up.

I spoke quickly. "Do you remember your family talking about a missing boy when you were small?"

Her eyes grew wide. "Oh, yes. I don't know who he was. The story was he turned up missing when his mother went in his room to get him. I had nightmares." She twisted her apron hem. "Aunt Annie, Gran, Mom—they'd all hush when I came in the room, but I heard snatches."

"What did you hear?" I held my breath, not wanting to miss a word or nuance in what she had to say.

"That he was gone and no one could find him. I used to have nightmares about gypsies."

"Gypsies? But they belonged to another time."

"Gran talked about gypsies stopping by to sharpen knives when she was a girl. When the little boy went missing, it made her think how she used to be afraid of them."

A stocky teenaged boy came through the door. He spoke to his mother and sat down at the counter.

"I have to go," said Irene.

"Thanks for your help," I told her.

Another waitress stopped at my table and asked if I wanted to order. Needing time to reflect on Irene's words, I ordered an iced tea and salad. She brought the tea, then the food, and I sat musing over a little red-headed girl with pale blue eyes listening to adults whisper about a small boy, whose mother discovered an empty crib when she went in his room.

But according to police, no one had reported a missing child. Fifty-plus years was a long time to keep records intact. Perhaps the report had been misfiled. I made a mental note to check the local newspaper archives.

Driving home, I mulled over Irene's information. Now I had corroboration that Edwina and Annie had spent months together in Spain. The fresh concept of hush money intrigued me.

Edwina had sent checks to Annie after she left Captain Frost's employ. Was the money given to encourage Annie not to tell about the baby or was it given out of a genuine concern for the Hendersons' welfare? I arrived home, exhausted from conjecture, but feeling I'd spent my evening well.

Mathieu was in the living room, talking on his cellphone. He didn't see me, so I eavesdropped. He told someone good night. Was he talking to Sybi? My hand went to my throat. After placing the phone on the coffee table, he disappeared into the half-bath. I grabbed his phone. A quick glance at his recent calls told me he'd been talking to someone at the Blue Spruce Inn, a local motel. I counted the calls—ten in all. They spanned the past six days.

The nightmare I'd suffered in Spain slammed into my mind. Was Sybi waiting for him at the motel? Had I caught him before he left for an assignation? As the bathroom door unlatched, I returned the phone to the table.

Mathieu looked startled to see me. "I didn't hear you come in, Maria."

He flashed an insincere smile. His posture—something was wrong there, too—he seemed tense, as if he didn't know which way to spring.

He kissed my hair. "Have you eaten? The Chinese is in the kitchen. I didn't get a chance to eat yet."

It was past nine o'clock.

His arms wrapped around me. Was that jasmine I smelled? Bergamot? His musk? I could no longer sort out the fragrances and broke away from him.

"I had a salad," I said, hearing the ice in my voice. "How—how have you spent your evening?"

He gestured toward his open briefcase on the sofa. "Grading papers. You?"

How could I make conversation with this man who was betraying me? It could not have been the first time. He'd been with Sybi before, kissing her lips, caressing her skin, covering her body with his—

Be calm, Maria. You don't know for certain he's been cheating.

"I drove to West Oak to talk to a waitress," I said curtly. "Her relative worked for Edwina. Tomorrow, I'm going to the newspaper office to search for references to a lost child."

"You've had a breakthrough. That's wonderful, Maria."

He turned me to face him. I moved away.

"What's wrong?" he asked. "You treat me like a leper."

"That's...too extreme," I protested, searching for something to say that would explain my behavior. "I-I'm still upset that I couldn't reach you when I was in Spain. I depend on you. I'm not comfortable traveling. I need to know that I can—"

"That happened weeks ago—"

"It still bothers me. You've never satisfactorily—"

"How can we lay this to rest?" he broke in. "I told you I didn't receive your calls. You know they don't go through down in the stacks."

I walked away from him. "You didn't even check your voice mail when I was abroad. I need you to be there for me."

He exhaled. "I did not check my voice mail." He opened his

hands in supplication. "For that you must forgive me, Maria."

I refused to be charmed. "Do you even love me, Mathieu?"

"Of course, I do. Why do you doubt me?"

An explosion of scents! Jasmine, bergamot, musk! I gasped.

"What's wrong?" he asked.

I coughed into my elbow crook, then said in a strangled voice, "Something has changed between us."

"You're the one who's brought change into our lives," he protested. "The biography increased your workload and—"

"And what?"

"You've become obsessed with the dead child. It's as if he were your own."

My arms hugged my body; I rocked back and forth. "That's absurd. I never wanted children."

"Maria, what is wrong with you? I've never seen you so agitated."

His phone rang, unstringing me. I sat down hard on the sofa. He picked up the phone. "Yes," he said, exiting into the kitchen. When he returned, he said, "A student, having trouble with his essay."

He was lying. I heard the sound of a car and jumped up to look out the window. Sybi was backing onto the street, leaving for her tryst with Mathieu. He placed his papers inside his briefcase.

"Maria, I didn't get a chance to tell you, but I need to meet a doctoral student at the library."

He was meeting Sybi! I gagged, then felt a swoosh of hellfire. Mathieu turned to me, a wall of flames between us. I heard Edwina's cackling voice: *See how betrayal hurts.*

I felt as if a vise were crushing my chest—then nothing.

Chapter XI

I woke on a gurney, feeling nothing. Mathieu held my hand loosely. Walls were tan and unadorned. I smelled the sting of antiseptic. Cold electrodes were slathered on my chest. A tall man in a white coat stood in the doorway.

"Maria," said Mathieu, tightening his grip on my hand. "I'm here, my love. You're in the hospital."

I blinked. The expression on his noble, dark face seemed reassuring.

"Just relax," he said. "No, don't try to sit up."

The man in the doorway spoke. "Has she been anxious lately, Dr. Joubert?"

"She's working on a book," answered Mathieu. "She just returned from Spain. Could she have contracted a bug?"

"I don't think so."

"Is it heart? Did she have a heart attack? She placed her hands on her chest, as if she were experiencing great pain."

"It doesn't appear so."

As they discussed me, I tried to look into Mathieu's eyes, but he was staring at the doctor. The memory of his infidelity returned. *Oh, Mathieu, you are the reason my heart suffers so.* But was that so? It wasn't certain I'd lost his love. My suspicion—yes, my *suspicion*—that he'd fallen in love with Sybi had put me under unbearable stress, but that hadn't been the cause of my chest pain. For that, Edwina was responsible.

I couldn't explain to my lover and to the doctor that I'd been in the grip of a malicious ghost.

"I want to do a MRI and a few other tests," the doctor said to Mathieu. "We'll schedule them for tomorrow. She'll be here for a couple of days."

A couple of days? I had to work on the book!

"Mathieu," I said weakly, "you must bring my laptop."

"No laptop," said the doctor. "You need rest."

"I have to search the newspaper archives."

"It's likely the earlier issues aren't digitized," Mathieu reasoned. "Give me your search words and I'll go to the newspaper office."

I struggled to sit up. "Yes, please. Check for references to the Bentleys, Frosts, Annie Henderson—"

"Maria, I insist you lie down," said the doctor.

Mathieu guided my shoulders onto the gurney and kissed my cheek. "Rest, Maria. I'll see what I can find."

I watched him walk off, his tall frame disappearing down the hallway. He didn't look back. What should I make of that? The doctor prescribed a sedative and I slept through the night.

* * *

Mathieu came next morning before a technician wheeled me away, then left afterward, once I was resettled in my room. The magnetic clinks and thumps of the MRI left me with a profound headache and I slept most of the afternoon. In the evening, Mathieu returned. His schedule had allowed only a couple of hours in the newspaper archives, but he planned to spend the next day there.

That night I couldn't sleep, and lay petulantly on a

starched white pillow, glaring at grotesque shadows on the wall. Around midnight—Edwina's perfume.

"It's past visiting hours," I said nastily, letting her know I was aware she'd caused the attack that sent me to the hospital.

No response.

"Go toward the light," I told her, directing her spirit to move on.

Though I spoke the words several times in the most commanding tone I could summon, her scent only grew stronger. For the first time, she manifested, appearing in a pale blue pixel state, which morphed into a quivering form. I had seen this transitioning before in séances, and was uneasy (because it was Edwina), but not afraid. Her face, as in life, expressed grimness. Then she mouthed the words, *Help me.* There was no utterance, but she'd made her meaning clear. I knew then her plight went beyond needing to make something right for the boy. Her soul was lost and she had latched onto me for some kind of assistance.

We gazed at each other, an otherworldly communion more intimate than any I'd had with living persons. I don't know how long she remained because she did not assert herself again and I fell asleep.

* * *

I didn't see Mathieu the next day until dusk had fallen. Though he'd spent eight hours at the newspaper archives, he found nothing about a missing child in Prophet County a half century ago. Instead, he brought copies of Frost and Bentley announcements, and I painstakingly went through them—a wedding, births, obituaries—then came to a photograph of a young Edwina standing in the crook of a tree branch with

William Bentley. It was an engagement announcement. How humiliating for Edwina that after telling the world of her love for Bentley, he'd abandoned her for her younger sister.

I segued to Sybi's attempts to take Mathieu from me. Only a day or two ago, I'd been certain they were having an affair. Now I wavered. As far as caring for me in the hospital, Mathieu had been constant, even loving. He'd put aside his article on voodoo to help with my research. I knew the article was important to him—it would be published in a leading scientific journal. My suspicion of his infidelity seemed to come and go.

"How awful for Edwina that Bentley jilted her after they announced their engagement," I remarked, looking quickly at Mathieu.

"I thought you'd find that interesting," he replied.

The engagement announcement was dated June, 1953—a year before Louise's child was born in Málaga.

"It's obvious he'd been cheating," said Mathieu. "Louise became pregnant and Bentley had to marry her."

"He probably fathered Edwina's baby, too." I said, in horror.

It was scandalous behavior, even in modern times. How had Captain Frost reacted? He had cloistered his daughters on his farm in an attempt to keep them from adverse influences and then—a fox had stolen into the henhouse.

If we posited that one of the babies, William or Joseph, ended up in the tool box, we were still short one child.

"It could be that William died at birth," I said. "I didn't think to ask for a death certificate for a child of Louise."

"There's still Joseph to account for," said Mathieu.

"As for Joseph, we know he didn't die in the hospital. I can't help but think he was renamed. Edwina would have given him another name, more in line with male names in her family."

"What's wrong with Joseph for a name?" asked Mathieu.

"The Frosts are Protestant. Joseph isn't the first name they would have chosen."

"Edwina could have given her child up for adoption," said Mathieu.

"Yes, that's right. I'm certain she never raised a child."

"But then who was in the tool box?" Mathieu's question was sobering.

We sat, neither of us speaking, for a time.

Then he broke the silence. "What do you know of Captain Frost?"

I shrugged. "Not much. He was an industrialist—possibly ruthless. According to Louise, he was away most of the time. In his photos, he looks like a tribal patriarch. He may have loved his wife; there's no mention of any romantic interest after her death. One of the Frost neighbors commented that he favored one of his female employees, but the only evidence she had was that he let the woman ride his horse."

He looked up quickly. "There could be sexual symbolism in that."

"And perhaps not."

"Maybe Edwina's child was kidnapped," said Mathieu. "I've read about the Lindbergh baby—how he was kidnapped and murdered. His body turned up in a wooded area not five miles from home."

I hadn't thought of kidnapping. "But wouldn't there have been publicity?"

"There was in the Lindbergh case, but Charles Lindbergh was a celebrity. Perhaps there had been threats on Frost's own children and that's why he moved to the country."

I had wondered, too, why Captain Frost moved to Prophet County, but upon learning of his wife's fragile health, guessed he'd wanted to settle where she could breathe fresh country air.

Mathieu gave me a sharp look. "Do you think Edwina knew the child was buried by the creek?"

I nearly said no, which would have been a mistake. I hadn't revealed to Mathieu that Edwina's ghost was—might be in the room listening to us.

"I don't think so," I answered.

"The little boy should be buried in hallowed ground," said Mathieu.

"First, someone has to claim him," I said. "It's been nearly six months since the bones were found."

"Was Edwina Frost religious?" Mathieu asked unexpectedly.

Her body of work contained religious overtones. Despite the gory aspects, her themes addressed juxtapositions of good and evil, as exemplified by Father Jean-Louis who scourged himself for sinful thoughts and murderous deeds.

"Her writing shows she was thoroughly immersed in Christian doctrine," I said firmly, "especially in matters of sin and redemption."

Our conversation had taken us away from the newspaper clippings. I sifted through them again.

"Where's Stuart's birth announcement?" I asked.

"I couldn't find it. I checked with the county clerk. There's no birth certificate on record for him."

No birth information for Stuart. What did that mean?

A loud speaker announced the end of visiting hours.

Mathieu piled the articles on my bedside table, leaned over, and kissed me. "You wear yourself out, Maria. Put away the clippings. You need to rest."

"Where are you going?" I asked, for I hadn't forgotten the Blue Spruce Inn and my nightmare that he and Sybi were lovers.

"Home, darling," he replied. "Why do you ask?"

If he was lying, he was glib. I turned to the wall. Sleep came in the small hours of the morning when shadows were blue.

Chapter XII

The MRI, CT scan, and EEG turned out to be normal, so the doctor released me from the hospital with a new prescription for antianxiety medication. Two days in the hospital had given me time to plan the next steps in my investigation into Edwina's past. I needed to talk to Louise Bentley and James Hawthorne again.

Louise was out of town. I drove to Otterbein to see James Hawthorne. He *had* to have known about Edwina's broken engagement and Louise's pregnancy—maybe even Edwina's. If I revealed that I knew about Edwina's child, I thought he might help me explain that part of her story with compassion. Something had happened to that baby—whether he was given away, kidnapped, or worse—and that loss certainly shaped her work.

James's bookshop was on Main Street in a renovated Victorian house with twin turrets. I spied him through a picture window, creating a display of Edwina's books. He appeared to be alone. As I stepped inside, a bell rang. I thought of the bell at St. Mary's Hospital.

He looked up. He was not pleased to see me.

"James," I said, beaming a smile. "I was driving by and thought I'd stop in."

"Are you interested in anything in particular?" he asked coldly. "I have a new anthology of Poe."

"Actually, I wanted to talk to you about Edwina. My research led me to Spain and the poet Ana Valencia. I learned Edwina had a son."

He paled.

"It was an important find," I hurried on, ignoring his reaction. "The loss of that child may well have caused her to see the world as unhinged, which, of course, was reflected in her fiction."

"Have-have you talked to Louise?" His voice sounded parched.

"Not yet," I said, "but I plan to soon."

He came toward me, his eyes wild. "You mustn't."

I stepped back. Just then the doorbell jingled furiously as a class of second or third graders came in. James gaped at them.

"Mr. Hawthorne, Mr. Hawthorne!" the children cried out.

I left, knowing James Hawthorne was privy to Edwina's secrets. Now I wondered if he was also privy to Louise's.

* * *

Saturday arrived and Mathieu left to play golf with friends. I dressed casually, in jeans and a grey sweat shirt, and then holed up in my study to read Anne Sexton, whose poems I planned to read aloud at a meeting of a poetry circle. As I perused "You All Know the Story of the Other Woman," something caught my eye—a dark flash, like a crow on the fly. I saw it again—a dark flicker at the edge of my peripheral vision. I adjusted the drapes, thinking it was a shadow from a tree. Edwina again? Was she trying to warn me away from the poem?

Too late. Sexton's theme flung Sybi Olivette into my consciousness. She was outside, trimming bushes, and I got up to look out the window. There she was, her flaming hair tied with a green scarf, sawing away at a hibiscus tree, five cats meowing at her ankles. I thought of Sexton's poem again: was Sybi the other woman or was I? If Mathieu was interested in her, how could I compete with that vitality, that intensity, that youth?

The cleaning lady knocked on the door. I released the drape, went downstairs, and let her in. She started the laundry and went upstairs to clean. Piles of soiled clothes lay sorted on the utility room floor. The whites sloshed inside the washer. The dark coloreds, which included Mathieu's trousers, were heaped near the doorway. He was notorious for not emptying his pockets. I lifted the top pair, his khakis, and put my hand in a pocket. A motel room key. Blue Spruce Inn. Room 207. I gasped for air.

Not this time. No anxiety attack. Keep calm.

Channeling South Sea breezes and white orchids, I laid the key on a shelf above the dryer. My heart broke. How could I deny Mathieu was sleeping with Sybi? Closing my eyes, I tormented myself with a vision of her lying on rumpled sheets, auburn hair fanned against a pillow, and Mathieu, lowering himself onto the bed, kissing her lips—

I couldn't bear it. Dashing out to the garden, I buried my head in my arms and sobbed. My life had never been so bleak. The cleaning lady left, slamming the door. In every sense of the word, I was alone.

I had built a sham life with my lover. I stared at our townhouse, our shelter from foul weather and thieves and neighbors—our sanctuary, where we'd made love, worked, cooked, and dreamed.

It had all been a lie.

Feeling like a protagonist in one of Edwina's novels, I fled, crossing the street into a park. A fat goose blocked my way. I kicked at it and it ran away. I hurried on. I'd believed Mathieu's love would last a lifetime, but I'd lost him to the amatory charms of a younger woman—something I'd always dreaded. Without him, I would have no bed mate, no one with whom to discuss nature, politics, and literature. Who would be my companion on trips—to Europe, to the Grand Canyon, to the grocery store? Who would I cook for or eat with? Without his love, my poetry, my life's blood, would dry up, for loving him had invigorated my writing. My man, my poetry, my soul—they were interwoven.

Now I would write of loss. I would be one of those poets who walked around with her pen connected to a black cloud.

Twilight settled with light rain. I ran through a schoolyard, tripping over uneven concrete, then the outer edge of a nature conservatory filled with bushes and trees. *Mathieu, how could you desert me? Do you wonder where I am? Are you worried about me?* Night fell. Lightning forked. The rain worsened and water pooled on the sidewalks. My fevered body cooled as rain drenched my clothing.

Plath's poems twisted in my head. I remembered her poem in which the "hag hands" of ancestresses reached out for her. I thought of Poe, Sexton, Teasdale. Did the latter pine for Vachel Lindsay, who ended his days drinking Lysol? I thought of a poem I'd written when I lost my first lover:

The galloping donkey—
Who sits astride
And uses the whip
That slashes the hide?

Oh rider—

Pursued by your phantoms
Which rotted inside,
Dreams came so quickly
And now have all died.

Trite, melodramatic. Unpublishable.

But the death of dreams was a terrible thing.

How could Mathieu love Sybi? She was such a shallow thing. What did they talk about, once they had exhausted the topic of monkey heads? Was this a night of lovemaking for them? I couldn't separate my tears from the raindrops. Was there a poem in that? I thought of all the words that rhymed with tears: fears, hears, nears, biers. But not biers, bier. A single death. My own.

I was going mad. I knew it. I followed a path under a viaduct where homeless people gathered in soiled clothing, bickering over scraps they'd filched from garbage cans. A shirtless man with a tattooed dragon on his bicep asked for money, but let me pass when I said I had none. A woman tried to barter my sweatshirt for a torn page from a tabloid. I told her no, kept walking, having no sense of purpose except to escape my entrapments. I continued on, stumbling over a crosshatch of railroad tracks, and passing old homes with plastic saints in the yards, auto repair shops, nail salons, a used car lot.

Clouds obscured the moon. I whispered poems—mostly Lorca's: *The moon, the moon is dead but in spring will come back to life and ...your face (ding dong) is simply a moonface (dong ding).*

When I again became aware of my circumstances, I was standing in a lighted parking lot at the back of the Bentley Hotel and Louise Bentley was unloading groceries from her car.

"Maria Pell," she said. "You gave me a start."

I had walked over ten miles.

Her eyes swept over my form. "You're soaked. You look like you could use a drink."

She thrust a grocery bag in my arms, took another for herself, and hurried toward the door. I stood dumbly, not sure what to do.

"Come on," she insisted. "You need help. You're not yourself, Maria."

I followed her meekly. Together, we rode the elevator to the top floor. She unlocked the door to her apartment, ordered me to shower, and gave me dry clothes. I obeyed her as if I were a child. When I came out of the bathroom, she poured brandy in two glasses.

"We'll go in the great room," she said. "You don't have to talk if you prefer not to."

Louise sat on the sofa. As always, she was dressed impeccably, this time in a forest green sheath and jacket. I wore her magenta tracksuit.

"Sit down," she said. "It hurts my neck to look up at you. I just returned from Florida. I've been opening the house."

I took the loveseat. "Hugh told me. Do you winter there?"

"I usually do. Hugh is planning his campaign, so I'll need to be here for part of the winter."

We were quiet, sipping our drinks. My body warmed. I recovered my senses.

"You're very kind to ask me up," I ventured. "I know you haven't been pleased with my research tactics."

"No, I haven't." She paused, then went on. "How's the biography coming?"

"I've finished six chapters and outlined the rest of the book—except for the final chapter."

Louise looked up at the ceiling. "We're all concerned about

that final chapter."

"Did you know Edwina was working on a novel when she died?"

"No. What was it about?"

"She had completed only seventy-three pages. It was the story of a seventeenth century Jesuit priest named Jean-Louis who went on a killing spree. Three times, she used the words, *who was not meant to be* in reference to the priest. I thought he might be a woman."

"Did the priest die?"

"She didn't finish the story."

"You'd be surprised at the number of times she killed me off in her books," Louise said wryly. "The priest is probably me."

We stared into our brandy glasses.

"Do you believe in spirits?" I asked.

"Do you mean liquor?"

"I mean the other kind."

She narrowed her eyes. "Don't tell me Edwina's been *haunting* you."

"I wouldn't say haunting. Sometimes I feel her spirit. I think it's lost."

"Don't let her suck you into her hell." Louise got up and refilled her glass. "More?"

Her hands were shaking.

"No, thank you. I went to Spain to talk to Ana Valencia."

"To Spain? Really?" Louise drank thirstily. "I didn't realize Ana was still alive."

"She's not doing well, but she remembered Edwina."

Louise resumed her seat, carefully placed the glass on a table, and sat with her hands tightly clasped. "How could she forget her? Edwina set her house afire. Her grandmother burned to death."

"What happened?"

"Edwina got drunk and was fooling around with a blow torch, of all things, in the atrium, trying her hand at metal sculpturing. She knocked over a kerosene lamp and the place went up in flames. The grandmother was asleep in her bed."

"I never read about it."

"Her agent covered it up."

Louise stared at the carpet. I finished my drink and wondered if Mathieu was home from his tryst. Heaving a sigh, I stood up, thanked Louise for her hospitality, and said I was going.

"I'll take you home," she said. "There's something I want to say."

We went downstairs, got in her car, and headed out the alley. We were quiet until we reached my townhouse.

"Thanks for everything," I said, my hand on the car door.

"Wait," she said.

I waited, eyebrows raised.

"All her life, Edwina hurt people," she said. "Our father paid people to hide her mistakes. Spending too much time with my sister could be harmful to your mental state."

Casting my eyes downward, I got out of the car.

"If you feel her near, sprinkle sage," advised Louise. "Keep some in your purse. After Will died, I used sage to keep him away."

Chapter XIII

Mathieu was asleep when I went inside. The motel key was gone from the laundry room shelf. He would think the cleaning woman had found it, but since it was lying in plain view, he would also wonder if I had seen it. I turned down the bed in the guest room and slept there, which would be answer enough. The next morning, I heard him in the shower, but remained in bed with my back to the door. As he went down the hall, he looked in briefly and then left the house, not bothering to eat breakfast. Hearing the front door close, I looked out the window in time to see him duck his head into the car.

After a light breakfast, I left for the university. My class met at eight and was over by eleven. I headed to my office and logged into the computer to find the address of the Blue Spruce Inn. I wasn't seized by a strong urge to go there, but wanted to be able to if I chose. Mathieu and Sybi wouldn't be there. He taught until six.

A student had asked to discuss a term paper topic. She arrived and we went over her notes on Antonio Machados's early work. When she left, I thought of the motel again, and was tempted to drive there—if only to see the location. Did I want to compromise my dignity by spying on my lover?

I did not.

I would not, should not—

Throwing good sense to the wind, I drove to the motel. The sign towered over a nest of spindly pines. I saw no spruces. The building was two-storied and painted teal with black shutters. Six cars were parked in the front lot.

Parking near the office, I climbed the stairs to the balcony. Room 207 was fourth from the end. I'm not sure what I intended to do—perhaps only look at the outside of the door. I heard voices—a woman's and a child's, speaking in a French dialect.

It wasn't Sybi in the room.

Mathieu wasn't cheating on me with Sybi at the Blue Spruce Inn.

What tremendous relief! Were the occupants of Room 207 his relatives from Togo? Why hadn't he told me they were visiting?

I started down the stairs. Then the door opened and a stoutly-built woman appeared, wearing a gold formless dress, which I recognized as a boubou. She saw me and said good morning, her voice a mixture of honey and grit. I murmured hello. She had European blood, as well as African, and her face was astonishingly beautiful; her skin was a lovely shade of bronze; her eyes bright green, her lips smiling. She wore her hair on top of her head, anchored with gold combs. A small boy darted in front of her.

I slunk away, got in my car, and watched as the woman knocked on the door of the adjacent room. A teen-aged girl stepped out. She, too, was dressed in a striking boubou. A taxi drove up. The woman and children went down the steps. As they reached the sidewalk, the woman's cellphone rang.

"It's Mathieu!" she called out.

My Mathieu!

"Come away from Mama Reine," the girl said to the boy.

Mama Reine? Who were these people to him?

For several moments, Mama Reine spoke on the phone. Then a cab pulled up, and they climbed into it and drove away.

Though I'd met some of Mathieu's relatives during our visits to Togo, I'd never seen these people. Who were they? Why had he kept their arrival a secret? Was he planning to return to Africa with them? Indignation fired my mind. I had loved Mathieu, shared my home, and been faithful to him for all our years together. I'd assisted him with his immigration status and introduced him to people who had furthered his career. Most importantly I'd given him time I could have been spending on my precious poems!

Clenching my jaw, I pursued the taxi into the countryside. It pulled into a rustic restaurant, used for university luncheons and dinners. The passengers got out. A man came out the restaurant door to greet them. I considered following them in, but then had second thoughts; if Mathieu was inside, I couldn't guarantee I'd behave. I might cause a scene and jeopardize both our careers.

Then reason cooled my fury. Perhaps there was another explanation Mathieu had the key. Perhaps the woman wasn't his lover, or even a family member. Since she was meeting people at this particular restaurant, her visit might be connected to the university. Perhaps she was a foreign academic and finding no one to care for her children, had brought them with her. Mathieu might have the motel key because he'd made travel arrangements for their visit. It might have been an extra key he forgot to give her.

She had called him Mathieu.

If she was a colleague, she would have done so. I called my colleagues by their first names. I felt ashamed.

Figuratively, I put on sackcloth and smeared ashes on my face. I went home and prepared a lovely dinner: flank steak stuffed with sage and breadcrumbs in a mushroom sauce. I baked a lemon meringue pie, Mathieu's favorite. Batting around the kitchen, I alternatively wept tears of relief and hummed tunes of joy.

Around six, Mathieu called to say he wouldn't be home until very late. Educators from Cairo were in town. A colleague tagged to take them to a meeting in Indianapolis and then to dinner, had fallen ill. Mathieu needed to step in. It crossed my mind that the woman staying at the motel might be among the educators.

Disappointed, I ate alone. After cleaning the kitchen, I sat on the sofa with Fritzi's head in my lap, petting her glossy fur, telling myself that Mathieu was where he said he would be. Indianapolis. A meeting, then dinner. Likely, there would be drinks afterward. Then I went upstairs and worked on Edwina's biography deep into the night. Finally too exhausted to tell a semi-colon from a question mark, I got in the bed I shared with Mathieu and kissed his pillow, knowing he'd soon be home. I slept peacefully, having resolved most of my concerns.

When the alarm went off at six, I discovered Mathieu was not beside me, nor was there a dent in the pillow I'd kissed. With Fritzi padding along behind me, I checked guestrooms. Empty. So were the sofas. Where was he?

I checked my cellphone. No recent calls. No messages on the answering machine. I dialed his number. No answer. Had he been in an accident? Was he asleep in someone's arms? Had he flown to Africa?

The dog barked. The front door opened and Mathieu entered. His jacket was torn, his shoes muddied. I ran to him, relief making me lightheaded. He caught me in his strong arms. He felt so good.

Then—a terrible wrench.

Edwina overtook me.

I pulled back from Mathieu. "Where have you been?" The utterance was nasal—Edwina's voice—not my own.

"Do you have a cold?" he asked.

"Why are you so late?" I demanded, in the same tone.

He rubbed his head. "It was a long night, Maria. The meeting lasted until three. I took four people home. One lives in the hills south of town and I got lost. I tried to turn around and got stuck in a mud hole. I waited hours for someone to come by to help me push the car out."

"I tried to call you," I twanged.

"My ringer must've been turned off."

"You turn it off when you don't want to talk to me!"

"I must have hit the sound button when I put the phone in my pocket. I don't do it deliberately."

Lies slid from his mouth like eels. I pierced him with my gaze and he averted his eyes. What an act he put on! Plunking himself down on the sofa, he made a great show of removing his shoes, complaining his ankles had been attacked by insects when he pushed the car from the mud hole.

"If you'd wear socks!" I shrieked. "Why didn't you call me?"

"It was late. I didn't want to wake you."

"Ha!"

"What's wrong with you?" He stared at me. "I came home as soon as I could."

"I don't believe you!"

My body shook with a simulation of rage; I owned it, yet I did not.

He raised his voice. "You don't believe me? Most of the night I was wandering around in one of your *hollers*, trying to find my way home to you!"

Then I felt my own self revive. His words, *find my way*

home to you, were like a poem. He loved me. I offered myself, wanting his arms around me again, but Edwina slammed in.

"Liar!" I cried, fixing him with a vicious glare.

I thought of all the nights I'd lain in his arms believing he loved me. I'd put up with Sybi falling all over him. And now he'd taken up with a woman from Africa, a woman whose skin shone like burnished metal, her eyes, like emeralds, her body, lush and—but no—

Hadn't I decided the African woman was a university guest?

Don't trick yourself, Maria. He's been unfaithful to you.

My eyes bore into Mathieu's. He *was* trying to trick me. He was having sex with the African woman. Why else would he have the key?

"You've been with someone!" I heard myself scream.

Hit him! Edwina's voice.

I raised my hand. Was I about to *strike* Mathieu?

He grabbed it. "What's wrong with you?"

"You betrayed me!"

Call him names!

"Liar! Bastard!"

Call him something African, then he'll understand!

"Jackal! Mongoose!"

Put a curse on him!

"Torment this man—"

"Maria!" cried Mathieu.

I thought of Reine, Mathieu's new love. It was she I should curse. Were her charms greater than mine? Colors flashed— red, black, purple—all dripping with hatred. I *yearned* to draw blood from the woman who'd exposed the last ten years of my life as a lie.

I wanted to kill.

Then words, the marrow of my life, failed me. All I could

voice were the sputter, gnashing, and beeps of—of crossed wires. Stumbling around the room, I spat unmerciful sounds —grr—rnch—sss. I heard a crow-like cackle. In a corner, Edwina loomed in her pixel state. *Kill. Kill. Kill.* I beat my fists on the table and shrieked: *I despise you, Will Bentley! I hate you and Louise and your little monster!"* My knuckles touched something soft, yielding. On the table was a sleeping form in light blue pajamas, a blond curly head. I heard a woman's desperate cry.

Billy!

I drew away.

A terrible silence, then Edwina: *Why won't you share?*

"Why won't you share?" I echoed.

"Share what?" yelled Mathieu. "You act like you're possessed!"

I was no longer Maria Pell. I had become Edwina. Lurching upstairs, I was a wind chime gone mad, clanging out a hellish dirge. A monster sat on my fiery brain digging her fingernails into my parietal lobe, jabbing at my spine. Unable to sit in a chair, I slammed around the room, back and forth, arms waving, knees buckling. Then the terrible music stopped. I grabbed the hem of my drapes and tore them, rod and all, from the window. I spewed the most profane words I could think of.

"Maria! Stop!" Mathieu shouted.

Seizing the letter opener from my desk, I lunged at him. He sidestepped, disarming me in the process. I snarled. He cried my name over and over.

Doesn't he know Maria is gone?

He pulled me into my rocking chair, held me tightly, and wept. Strange—his tears offered release—an offering to some savage god—perhaps far off on an African veldt. Exhausted, I leaned against him. He rocked the chair, perhaps for hours.

The rhythm consoled me. I closed my eyes, completely spent.

I awoke later in our bed, smelling jasmine. Electrical charges pulsed blue in the dark. Mathieu was talking on the phone in his study. Who was he talking to? Men in white coats, to take me away?

I could do that myself.

I went into the bathroom, opened the medicine cabinet, and swallowed all my medication.

Chapter XIV

I opened my eyes. My throat felt raw, my eyes, unfocused. Mathieu's voice. "Maria. You'll be all right. They've pumped your stomach."

His face was featureless. Was I in hell?

"What-what is this place?" I asked.

"You're in the hospital."

"I can't see." I said, my voice hoarse. But it was *my* voice, not Edwina's.

"Some of the drug is still in your system. The blurred vision will pass."

I hated it, the wavy lines of the door frame and windows, the trembling crucifix on the wall.

He kissed my forehead, whispering, "Why did you want to die when I love you so much?"

I lay still, not answering. My bones felt rubbery, my muscles limp, like those of an infant. My mind was exhausted. Was Edwina gone? I thought she was. Would Mathieu understand if I said it was she who had taken the pills? I made slits of my eyes, trying to see him. His posture was slack, as if he were on the verge of giving up.

No, he wouldn't understand. I dozed off.

When I woke, he was still sitting beside the bed.

"Mathieu," I said.

"I love you," he said, his voice almost a groan.

I didn't know if that was true. But my feelings for him, steady, true, *infinite*, pushed thoughts of Edwina into an abyss. He reached over to touch my hand and I fumbled for his palm, his fingers. Quickly, he clasped my hands in his. I fell asleep.

* * *

In the morning, I awoke to the sight of a well-dressed woman seated beside the bed. I frowned, trying to see her face. Louise Bentley.

"How long have you been here?" I asked in little more than a whisper.

"A half-hour or so," she said softly. "Hugh told me you were here."

Mathieu had apparently informed Hugh that I'd tried to kill myself. Hugh would be discreet—it might affect his campaign.

"Where's Mathieu?"

"He went to the cafeteria. What a nice man he is, Maria. So devoted to you."

"Yes, it would seem."

"I told him I wanted to save you from Edwina. It wasn't you who took those pills. It was she."

Astonished that Louise understood, I turned on my side to get a better look at her. Tears fell as I remembered my episode of madness when Edwina gained possession of me. I'd tried to kill Mathieu, whom I loved more than life. Edwina had asked— why won't you share? She'd wanted me to share her guilt. I'd felt my fists on the child. Had I struck him? No, I had not followed her on that twisted path.

Louise's voice broke into my thoughts. "Mathieu said this is the second time you've been in the hospital since beginning work on the biography. Can't you see Edwina means to destroy you? Give up the book. Keep the advance."

I looked at her. She stared back. We had shared a common experience—Edwina—and belonged to a battered sisterhood. I saw how false reasoning had led me, not to scholarship, but to Edwina's scheme to involve me in the killing of her nephew. My hair fell in my eyes, and I brushed it back.

"Tell me about the boy in the toolbox," I said.

She looked down at her rings. "You must swear to secrecy."

I nodded.

"What has your research turned up about us?" she asked.

"Edwina's fiancé, William Bentley, seduced you when you were sixteen. He had sex with both of you during the same time period. You and Edwina conceived sons and were delivered of them two months apart in Spain."

Her eyes filled with tears, but none spilled over. "How tawdry it sounds. But yes, that's what happened. Go on."

"I'm not sure what happened after that."

Tears ran down her cheeks. She wiped them away, and took a deep breath. "The child in the toolbox was my little Billy." Her eyes bore into mine. "Will and I went to Spain for his birth, as you know. Father was so disgusted with us, particularly with Will, that we sought a peaceful place for my confinement. We had gone to Málaga on our honeymoon, so we went back there. Edwina told no one she was pregnant with Will's child. She went on a European tour. I suppose she had her boy in Málaga because I had Billy there."

"Did you and Will return to Fennville after Billy's birth?" I asked.

"Father forgave us—he finally had a male heir. We set up housekeeping. Then Edwina came back with her son, telling Father she'd married an Italian count and he was the boy's father. Her first night in Fennville, she came to visit. James was there. He'd come to ask Will's help with a financial matter. My husband was sitting in an armchair, holding Billy. Edwina accused him of fathering her son. Will denied it, but she described places and dates of their rendezvous." She shook her head. "I was ignorant—I hadn't known."

"You were very young," I said quietly.

"Edwina flew at them—Will and Billy—before we could stop her. Though I've always thought she meant to strike Will, her fists fell on my little one's head and—"

She broke off. I pitied her. She sat for several moments, wiping her nose, drying her eyes.

"James grabbed her. Will stood up, holding Billy. Blood was—"

James Hawthorne had tried to stop Edwina—that explained his behavior.

Louise bowed her head. "I...I went to Billy and took him from Will. I remember sitting down and holding him close. If he had any last breaths in him, he died in my arms." She shook her head, as if to clear away thoughts so painful she could not bear them. "Father insisted we cover it all up. He took Billy's body and said he'd bury him. He didn't say where. I was distraught—"

He buried him by the bridge on a dark, dark night and threw the shovel in the stream.

"What happened to Edwina's son?" I asked softly.

"Father made her give him to me," she whispered.

An eye for an eye.

I was shocked. Captain Frost had found an Old Testament solution. I forced myself to imagine the family drama: a child dead, at the hands of his aunt; a young mother, witness to his death; a weak man, the cause of it all; the outraged captain of industry, and the killer, condemned to live out her days recapturing the moment in prose. Then another devastating blow—Frost forced Edwina to give her son to Louise.

I understood the dynamics, but to understand the pain, I would need to be mad. Edwina had given me that unwelcome gift yesterday and I lay in a hospital bed, as a result.

My eyes drifted to Louise, who sat so perfectly coifed and groomed, a woman who was no stranger to despair, yet carried on with dignity. To say I'd gained a new respect for her was an understatement.

"Edwina had called her boy Joey," Louise went on. "I renamed him Stuart, my husband's middle name. He resembled Billy—they had the same eyes. The substitution of one little boy for another was relatively easy." She tilted her head toward me. "I told friends we'd decided to call him Stuart to avoid confusion with two Williams in the family."

Outside, the wind rose. We both turned our heads toward the window.

I broke the silence. "Louise, why did your father bury Billy by the creek?"

She shook her head. "I don't know. He'd never tell me where he'd buried him, saying it would only make me miserable to visit the grave. I was horrified when I learned a child's skeleton was found by the creek. I knew it was Billy."

"What did Edwina say happened to her own son?"

"No one here knew she'd had a child except Annie Henderson, who'd gone with her to Spain. She told Annie that her husband, the count, had carried him off." She paused. "It warped Edwina, of course, what she'd done. She was already a damaged soul. Perhaps if there had been a trial, an opportunity for her to prove it was an accident, but no—Father didn't want the publicity. We sealed it all in our minds."

She and I sat quietly for a while. The hospital sounds—voices, beeps, rattling trays—seemed far away.

"Will you claim Billy's remains?" I asked hesitantly.

"I *want* to bury him in the family plot, but there's Hugh to consider. To reveal that his brother was murdered by his aunt, who had been impregnated by his father—that would be a catastrophe for his political aspirations. I'm forced to think of the living." She glanced at me quickly. "Don't you agree?"

I thought of the Episcopal cathedral downtown.

How easy it was to become a co-conspirator.

"Couldn't Hugh persuade the authorities to release Billy to you?" I asked. "Then you could bury him in a crypt in the cathedral."

She leaned toward me. "Wouldn't the press figure it out?"

"Plant an item in the local paper. Something noble: *the Frost family has given refuge to the child found on their property. Reinterment will take place on such-and-such date...*"

I saw a light of hope in her sad eyes. "I hadn't thought of that. Perhaps..."

"Does Hugh know Stuart was Edwina's son?"

"No. There was no reason to tell him." She glanced at me. "I want to keep that from him."

Hugh Bentley could be thick-headed, but he wasn't stupid.

"If you reinter Billy's remains, he'll ask why you're doing it."

"You're right. I must think about it."

We smiled at each other.

"I almost forgot," she said, reaching into her purse for a small envelope. The pungent odor of sage filled my nostrils as she scattered it around my bed.

"Do you truly believe it will keep Edwina away?" I asked.

Louise kissed my forehead. "I *know* it will. Maria, I hope you'll abandon the biography. No good can come of it."

I envisioned an eager graduate student, a fan of Edwina's fiction, persuading a committee to give her a grant and tracing her beloved author to Spain. Edwina's relationship with Ana Valencia would lead to Málaga, and possibly the birth records stored at St. Mary's Hospital. I could see the blurb: *Queen of Horror Fiction Killed Baby Nephew.*

"Let me think about it," I said.

The vacation in Tuscany was fading.

Chapter XV

Mathieu took me home from the hospital the next day. Fritzi shied from me. Had I mistreated her when I was in Edwina's clutches? The house reeked of sage. I lay on the sofa while he tucked an afghan around me.

"In case you have not noticed," he said, "I have strewn sage throughout our home."

"Did Louise give it to you?"

"She gave me the idea, but I purchased it. In bulk."

"Thank you."

"No need to thank me. If you had told me Edwina's ghost was interfering, I would have thought of it immediately. It is a voodoo practice. My mother used to purify our home with herbs." He regarded me gravely. "Why didn't you tell me Edwina was haunting you?"

I squirmed. "I knew how you felt about restless spirits. I was afraid you'd ask me to give up the biography."

"That would have been good advice."

"Yes. I'm sorry, Mathieu."

He heaved a long sigh. "I know you visit the spirits of departed poets. I'm not sure—"

"You must leave me my poets."

"Can you keep them in their places?"

"Yes. Yes, I'm sure I can."

He nodded. "Is Edwina gone, do you think?"

I sniffed the air. A faint odor of sage. When Mathieu came close, I smelled musk.

"She's gone," I said.

Was it the sage that drove her away? Or had my return to sanity done it? Or had Louise's tentative plan to bury her son in hallowed ground? Or had Mathieu's demonstration of love? Perhaps, all these things came together so powerfully that Edwina could no longer assert her will.

Throughout my ordeal, Mathieu had shown love and support. It did not seem that he intended to leave me, but the time had come to speak of the African woman and what she was to him. I summoned my courage.

"Please tell me about the woman at the Blue Spruce Inn," I said.

He sat down. Leaning forward, elbows on knees, he stared at his shoes. He lifted his head and looked at me. "You saw the key."

"Yes and I drove to the motel."

"You saw Reine and Yvette and little Emmanuel?"

"Who are they? Colleagues? Family?"

"Reine is my former wife, Yvette is my daughter, and the boy is Reine's son with another man. She came to ask my blessing because she wishes to marry the father."

His former wife? He had a daughter named Yvette? He'd never spoken to me of a wife and child. I'd assumed from what he'd told me of his past, he'd always been single—a scholar, struggling to earn his doctorate. On our trips to Togo I'd met his parents, a sister, cousins—

"I'm confused, Mathieu. Your family never mentioned your ex-wife and child."

"No, they would not. They would not want to harm our relationship."

"Do you have contact with your daughter?"

"Reine and I parted when Yvette was very young. She found another man to love when she studied in Egypt. Yvette accepted him as her father."

"You could have told me about them. You could have told me they were here."

"I should have told you when we first met, but I was afraid you'd leave me. As time passed, I kept silent because I feared you would think me deceptive for not telling you earlier."

"You put yourself in a trap."

"Yes, a trap. Then Reine decided to time her request for my blessing with a conference at the university. You seemed to distrust me around Sybi, and I worried how you would feel about Reine coming—especially since I had never told you about her. As you became more involved with the dead boy, you got farther away from me and I was afraid—"

I frowned. "Where are Reine and the children now?"

"They've returned to Egypt. I gave my blessing to her new marriage. We will never see them again if that is your wish."

"I don't know that's necessary—"

"We can discuss that later, Maria. It will be up to you, but now I want to talk about what happened with Edwina's spirit."

His abrupt switch from the topic of an ex-wife and child registered. Still, since I had tried to kill him, he would want to know why.

"She fed my insecurities and broke my will. In the beginning, I welcomed the opportunity to communicate with her—I sought desperately to understand her—" Tears were coming; I blinked them back. "It was a classic case of possession."

Remembering the darkness of that time, I bowed my head.

"Look at me, Maria."

I raised my head.

He stroked my shoulder. "I witnessed the effect Edwina's spirit had on you. I know of possession. I saw it in Togo." His black eyes riveted me. "But we must have no more of your uncertainty about my devotion to you. My heart is yours. I am like the antelope struck by the hunter's spear. I belong only to you."

I bit my lip. "I'm sorry, Mathieu."

He kissed me, then said, "Now while I prepare our dinner, come sit in the kitchen. You haven't told me Louise's story. I want to hear it."

While he cleaned vegetables for the pasta, I told him the tragic story of Billy Bentley's death.

When I finished, he said, "Finally we come to the end of this dark tunnel. When Louise lays Billy's bones to rest, Edwina will find peace. Her debt to this world will be paid."

"I hope so," I said.

"It will be so."

* * *

In the end, I chose not to write Edwina's story. After returning the advance to Hugh, I burned all my notes and deleted everything from my hard drive. I gave Edwina's unfinished manuscript to Louise. She poured brandies and we watched as she burned it in her fireplace.

"Was that book going to be about me?" she asked.

"It was about Edwina," I answered. "All her books were about herself."

If graduate students down the road wanted to write about Edwina Frost, they'd have to start from scratch. Time would soon reduce the number of witnesses to Edwina's story to zero.

* * *

The day after Hugh Bentley announced his run for state senator, I received a phone call from Louise.

"Maria, I'm inviting you and Mathieu to a funeral mass for Billy. I want you to sit with us."

"A mass? You're going to reveal who Billy is?"

"I wish I could, but I have to think of Hugh. Although we're burying Billy in our family plot, we will refer to him, as far as his monument is concerned, as *Child*."

"I see."

"As you suggested, we'll release a statement, saying the Bentley family is giving rest to the unknown child." Louise sighed. "That will give me some measure of...I suppose...peace. It's unrealistic to expect closure on something like this."

She didn't say it, but she had outlived two sons.

That was the thing about Louise—she didn't seem to feel sorry for herself.

At the next Planet Savers meeting, I sat next to Hugh Bentley. His demeanor was expansive, as befitted a senatorial candidate. After the meeting, he embraced me warmly. Neither of us spoke, but his impulsive act told me his mother had informed him of Billy. And, of course, if he knew about Billy, he knew about Stuart.

In retrospect, I think Hugh sought me out to acknowledge that I held his fate in my hands. An uncommon act of humility, I thought. He knew he could trust me.

Epilogue

The community had become swept up in the story of the child whose bones were found on Frost property. The turnout for Billy's funeral mass was nearly as large as the one for Hugh Bentley's victory party when he won the state senate seat several months later. Louise attended both events, of course, dressed in black for the funeral mass and in Republican red for the celebration. At the funeral, I sat in the row behind her, and as I stared at her chic haircut and silk-covered shoulders, I sensed her relief. No doubt, she had shed a river of tears for her little son, as she had later for Stuart, when he was killed by a sniper. She had been able to bury Stuart, and now could do the same for Billy.

As the priest spoke, I flipped open my notebook to find the poem I'd begun after Edwina's interment. From time to time, I'd worked on it, adding and deleting words, breaking lines differently. I'd added a bit about Cardinal John Henry Newman, who was born into the Romantic era of Keats and Shelley. In 2008 when Rome was considering the cardinal for sainthood, his coffin was opened so his remains could be entombed in Birmingham Oratory. But there were no remains. Had they vanished because his wooden coffin had disintegrated? Was it because of the damp earth surrounding the grave? Or was it something else? One expert said if conditions were such that the bones disintegrated, so should the handles on the coffin, which were extant. The good cardinal wouldn't mind sharing a poem with Billy.

Bones

Did you want my lovely bones?
Beneath this earth is a grave spaded

deep for your beloved. And if my bones
should vanish without trace like Cardinal Newman's,

believe them there anyway, for who needs bones?
Those requiring relics can find photos of hanks of hair,

cloth from shrouds, or even fleshed out fingers.
Did I not see St. Thomas's in Italy?

Bones, holy in their silence, received the kiss
of the Bridegroom at the last mass
and that was enough.

Billy Bentley's bones lay in hallowed ground at last.

Made in the USA
Charleston, SC
25 April 2016